Contents

Book Description

I came back to Ambrosia to ascend the throne after my father abdicates. It is supposed to be a smooth process, I am already engaged to a princess from one of the four kingdoms, what I don't expect is the minx sent to masquerade as my mistress. She tempts me and makes me feel things I haven't felt in a long time. I am at peace whenever I am with her and she puts a lot of my plans at risk, but is it a risk I am willing to take?

Edward Vaughn hasn't lived in Ambrosia, the kingdom he was born and raised in, the kingdom of the gifted since the death of his mother.
He was sent away for his protection by his father and he has now been summoned back to ascend the throne.

Since returning, his gifts and powers are out of control and for someone who can heal himself, he keeps on having migraines.

The only time he is at peace is when he is with Leilani.

His keeper, his greatest weakness, his muse and his downfall.

Acknowledgments

Thank you Lu, for believing in me and encouraging me to do what I live the most.

Dedication

To you the readers who despite not knowing me have decided to take this journey with me.
Thank you.

Places

Kingdom Ambrosia
Kingdom Pelrise
Kingdom Fairah
Kingdom Quewest
Independent Islands

Terms

Keeper - A special royal guard either born with keeper blood or selected at the birth of a royal.
Gifted - A person born with supernatural abilities

Chapter 1

Edward Vaughn

I watched another flower die, a rose this time around. I watched it wither and die at a rate and speed that could never be considered normal. I felt a slice of pain travel up my arm even as I breathed heavily, gasping for air.

" I can't father." I said, wheezing out the words to my father, Ambrose Lennon, the king of Ambrosia.

" You can, you're just not trying hard enough Edward." he says and from the sound of his voice, I can tell he is getting frustrated,

" Try again." He says to me.

I pick up another rose, a red one this time. It's still fresh and alive, it smells like the gardens mom likes to have her picnics in. I hand the still fresh rose to father, he takes it and as always I watch in awe and silence , as the rose in his hand goes from fresh and alive, to dead and dry in a matter of seconds.

He makes it seem so easy but I know it had to take a little power out of you, turning something that was once beautiful and vibrant into something that can be turned to dust at the flick of a finger.

He hands the rose back to me and I take it, holding it delicately because I know any slight mistake and it would be nothing more than crunched up dry petals.

I breathe in and close my eyes like father has taught me, then I let all the power in me flow through my hand to where I was delicately holding the flower.

I feel a slight tingling sensation in my palm and I open my eyes.

I see a small bright light glowing in my palm, like that of the night flies that I always see from my wing in the castle.

I feel life start growing back in the rose, it's petal getting back the water and life father had drained earlier.

I see it start to bloom again under my touch, it starts to open up and grow and I breathe in a sigh of relief, my heart skipping a happy beat as I look at the flower.

Just as quickly as it had begun, the glow from my hand goes out like a candle that has been snuffed out and I watch the flower die faster than it had before when father had held it. Its petals dry up faster than the ones before. Fuck!

I throw the damn flower away and punched the table, breaking it in the process.

" Patience is a virtue Edward, one that we unfortunately don't have at the moment." Father says and I feel my heart stopping and returning back to normal from the galloping pace it was going at.

"Go to sleep. Come back here first thing in the morning, I will have the servants bring in more flowers so you can continue to practice." He tells me before leaving. He was probably in a rush to go back to mom,

" Yes father." I answer though I have no intention of going to sleep anytime soon though I made sure to keep my thoughts hidden.

" And Edward," father calls, stopping just outside the door of the room where we had all of our practices and sessions,

" Yes father.",

" Remember, I also didn't get it right the first time around, it took alot practice." He tells me before closing the door.

I kneel down and sigh, he had all the time he needed at the time he needed it but like he said I didn't have any or any patience left for that matter.

He was two hundred and thirty-eight years of age and when he had started learning to heal, my late grandfather, the greatest and most powerful in our line, had been the one to teach him. He had all the time in the world then because then, we lived openly among the mortals but now we had to hide for fear of exposure would lead to one of us ending up in some science lab somewhere. Although I knew I was the only one in danger, not him. I was fifteen years of age and it was becoming very clear that I was bad at hiding who I was. Every time I got a cut or broke my fingers when boxing with my friends, I was healing faster and my wounds and cuts were healing and closing within seconds.

Father had noticed of course and had started teaching me the art of healing and delaying healing. It had all gone well for most part, I had learnt to delay my healing process long enough so as not to raise suspicion and answer uncomfortable questions like why the fingers that had been clearly broken the door before were all fixed the following day.

The one thing that kept on giving me issues though was healing, we have started small hence the roses, if done right the healing is permanent but if done wrong, the effects were irreversible.

I came from a long line of gifted royals, the most powerful mortals to ever exist in all the four kingdoms. Centuries ago, we lived among the mortals, free and not hiding but as the years went by, mortals wanted what the royals had.

Power.

Through developing and growing, they started building machines and making labs and stealing samples from anyone of the royal bloodline trying to recreate what was never theirs to begin with.

Obviously it didn't end well, the few mortals that managed to get a bit of the power they sought couldn't control it. It instead consumed them, became bigger than them and turned them against each other.

They decided to fight the royals, and like in every war. They were casualties.

All royal families from all four kingdoms, Ambrosia, Pelrise, Fairah and Quewest, died along with a few mortals.

My grandfather died but my father somehow survived.
The other kingdoms, mortals took over control of the thrones and started to rule but father has been ruling Ambrosia for two hundred years, taking different names and forms, getting married none the wiser, he of course has never had children apart from me.
To everyone else around the four kingdoms, history is a load of bullshit and no war ever happened.
They think it's some myth or legend and I never bother to correct them.
The only other people aware of my and my father's identity are the royal keeper top five,the ones that are trusted with it. They are trusted because they are the second most powerful mortals on earth, capable of controlling the four elements of the earth, they can block mind control, power of flight and power absorption.
They are sworn to protect royals till their dying breath. The last true royal guard is Gareth Hayes and my personal guard.
I check the time on my watch and curse. Fuck. It is almost midnight meaning I had been learning to heal for eleven hours straight. I get up to go and shower.
After my shower, I am about to go to bed when I hear something smack my window. I smile to myself, already knowing who it is without even checking. Mabel Hope. My only friend or girlfriend in this case though no one knows. She is the only child who lives within the caste grounds because her older brother Donovan Hope is part of the royal guards.
A promising young talent, Gareth had called him which says a lot because Gareth doesn't compliment anyone.
There are guards standing outside my door and down the wall below my window which makes it hard to sneak out but now impossible.
I wear some sweatpants, a hoodie and sneakers. I call all the power within me and concentrate on my skin, turning on my invisibility gift, opening the door and wall right past the guards outside my door.

Lionel, one the guards, looks right through me as I open and close and close the door but doesn't suspect a thing.
I go down the long corridor, go through the door that is reserved for guards and go out into the garden. Once outside, I shift back and I am visible again before breathing in the polen filled air.
It's a cool and clear night out meaning I can see the stars and there happens to be a full moon. I don't linger though, knowing that a guard might pass by patrolling so I make my way to one of the ponds and find Mabel sitting by the water, waiting for me.
Her hair is in braids as always and her black skin shining against the moonlight glow.
She hears my approach and turns, looking at me and smiling.
" I thought you forgot about me, Edward." She says teasingly,
" As if I could ever forget about you. Sorry, time got away from me, I had a training session with father today." I tell her taking a seat next to her.
" Another training session, is there a war we should know about?"
She asks me jokingly and I just laugh it off awkwardly. I read her mind and get nothing from her but genuine curiosity. She gets something wrapped in foil from her pocket and hands it to me,
" Eat this. I doubt if you even remembered to eat during your session." She tells me.
I want to argue with her when my stomach growls so I just take it and unwrap it, finding a roasted drumstick. I take a bite, moaning a little at the crispy, crunchy deep fried skin and she laughs at me.
" When are you taking me out on my date. I am getting tired of waiting you know,"
she asks me, changing topics. A tactic I have seen her use on me.
Mabel's parents died in a fire the year before, the fire killed about fifty people. No knows the cause if the fire till date, the fire department and police departments of Ambrosia not knowing the cause sort of made it a closed case.
Her older brother Donovan took her in and has been raising her since but it hasn't been easy. She is the only one who survived

the fire though no one knows how because nothing could be salvaged from the building and the houses surrounding it.

" How about tomorrow, I will come and pick you up around 8pm and then we can watch a movie or something." I tell her.

" That sounds nice."

Is the only response I get but it doesn't bother me because like I said, before anything else Mabel is my only friend just like I am hers.

We sit and watch the fish swim, hear the crickets chirping and talk about school and how her training is going because she plans to join the royal guard.

She has been preparing for the try outs that the royal guard hosts for all eighteen year olds interested, which are a lot. Ambrosia is a rich kingdom, the richest of all four kingdoms recalls meaning all careers pay well but the royal guard have the best pay.

Which in part is why so many people want to join it's forces but very few get in. She is very excited and hopes she gets in, the last time someone below the age eighteen got in, it was her brother who is now twenty. I hope she gets in though.

We sit and talk till my ass gets numb because of sitting on the hard ground when I finally escort her back to her brother's apartments.

I sneak into my room and sleep for the four hours before waking up and going back to practice my healing.

" Fuck!!!!!" I scream, frustrated with myself and the damn flowers. I came here to practice first thing in the morning.

Like father had said, I found dozens of roses waiting for me, dead ones just to be clear. I have been trying to bring at least one to life and all my attempts have gone in vain.

My temper has gotten the best of me once again because there

is yet another broken table in need of replacing. My only saving grace today is the fact that father isn't here to witness this.
The door opens and mom steps in, looking as graceful and radiant as she always does.
" Such language is unbecoming for a prince." She tells me as a way of greeting. I smile sheepishly and I sigh.
" I am sorry, I have had a tough morning." I tell her, standing up from where I have been kneeling. My mother, father, Gareth and Leilani are the only people that I am ever at peace with. When I am with any other person or around a lot of people in general, my head hurts alot which is weird because nothing can hurt or kill me.
But being around people is like going out in the middle of a storm, you get hit everywhere at once by forces of nature except for me I am hit with everyone's thoughts all at once. Mortals are not good, they always expect something in return and if I was asked to save a life between mortal and animal I would pick animal.
" Vaughn, it's past 1pm. You have been here since 6am and quite frankly son, you stink. You need to rest." Mom tells me, interrupting my thoughts. I act wounded at her words,
" Mom, I do not stink. The stench you smell is that of power and wasted effort." She rolls her eyes at me,
" Well I for one am glad I don't have the power you do then." She tells me, going to open the windows. Only after the windows are open do I internally agree with her, fresh air and the air in my room are very different.
" Come and have tea with me, we can paint and you can go for a swim. You haven't had time to relax ." She gently asks me.
I sense her worry but I can't go out, not yet at least.
" I can't today, I am not even close to learning to heal mom and I need to learn. It's the last of gifts that I haven't learnt to control yet.",
" And you will, in good time. Vaughn, you learnt how to control your shape shifting, how to control your strength, your imperceptibly. You will find your healer's touch as well but I just

don't want to stop taking care of yourself in the process."
Her words are spoken softly but I can sense the anger in them,
" I am taking care of myself." I tell her,
" Really, well then your highness, when was the last time you had a proper meal?" Fuck.
I know I am in shit has hit the fan when she addresses me as your highness because she only ever calls me Vaughn, not Edward or my prince or your highness just Vaughn.
" I had a drumstick last night." I say as a last resort because she is right. Whenever I start to learn a new ability or to unlock a gift, I stop concentrating on anything else other than my gift. I am not a good multi-tasker.
" Right, a chicken drumstick solves everything." She says sarcastically and I almost laugh but hold it in before it gets out.
" Vaughn, I am your mother and I care about you. Go and take a shower or a bath and meet me in the rose garden in twenty minutes for tea."
She tells me in a voice that leaves no room for arguments.
She leaves and I follow her out, her going to the gardens and me going to my rooms. She walks with the grace of someone who was born a royal even though she only married into royalty. I am not sure with the specifics exactly. All I know is that father met her at the opening of one of the local schools, fell in love and well here I am.
I shower quickly, get dressed and go out to meet mom in the rose garden. The rose gardens are reserved only for members of the royal family and they are her favourite part of the palace.
We sit there and paint together on most days or she sits and reads a book while I swim.
Servants and guards here and there offer some your 'highnesses' as a way of greeting but I don't stop to address them, I simply walk past them. I only stop When I find Gareth waiting for me by the door.
" Your highness." He says as he bows.
" You may rise Gareth." I tell him, sounding indifferent. I start walking towards the gardens and he falls in step beside me,

" How many times have I told you not to bow and to simply call me Edward?" I ask him a little frustrated.
" I don't know your highness, I stopped counting when you turned fifteen."
He answers and I can hear the laughter in his voice. I don't have to read his thoughts to know that he addresses me by my royal title and a way to piss me off.
" Haha, very funny."
I tell him sarcastically. We walk in silence passing more guards along the way. The royal family of Ambrosia has the most insane security detail, so there are cameras and armed guards at every corner. Watching.
That's one of the reasons I always wear a hoodie whenever I sneak out with Mabel.
" I came to your room last night." Gareth's voice startles me, once again breaking all my thoughts.
" You weren't there. Which I find very confusing because you know, the guards outside your door were so convinced that you were inside your room, sleeping like you were supposed to." Ah fuck.
" I went out, I was tired and I wanted some fresh air." I lie.
" And you couldn't get said air with security?" I stop walking and look at Gareth, pissed for the invasion of privacy and why the fuck he is questioning me when I am his prince.
" I went out, you don't have the right to question what I did or who I did it with. Your job is to protect me, not question my decisions and choices." I tell him looking him straight in the eyes as I do that. He bows slightly and i know that i have fucked up once again,
" I'm sorry, your highness. But I am paid to protect you, I swore an oath to protect you so it is my job to know where you are at all times." Ah fuck.
Gareth is my friend though he will never admit it and he is like a second father to me.
I have never questioned him or used my power over him but I have had a rough morning. We continue walking in silence until

we reach the garden.

I find mom with Leilani, another member of the royal guards and mom's friend. No one knows she is a member of the royal guard though, only a select few. She is like an undercover spy whose sole purpose is to protect mom.

" Good afternoon, your highness." She greets me bowing,

" Good afternoon Leilani. You may rise."

I greet her. Mom smiles proudly as she sips her tea. I walk over to where she is seated, painting on a large canvas.

" What are you painting today?" I ask her, looking at the blank canvas she has in front of her.

" I haven't decided yet, I am waiting for inspiration I guess." My mother is a talented artist, while me and my father have these amazing and powerful gifts, she paints and draws. I guess I got some of my artistic skills from her but I am nowhere near as good as she is.

" Ok, let me swim a few laps before I can join you."

She nods her head distractedly, so I fake off my clothes, remaining with my swim trunks. Gareth moves to sit a few feet closer to the pond. I jump into the pond, shivering a little at the cold water before I start swimming. I can hear mom and Leilani's voices as they laugh and talk about Lord knows what.

Mother likes to make these picnics for me whenever she knows I have training with father. She says I need to be a kid despite being royal and the heir to Ambrosia and father thinks that I need to concentrate on my lessons and training sessions with him. Today isn't the first time she has told me to leave my lessons and just 'relax' for a while.

I am in the middle of my fourth lap around the pool when I hear gunshots ring out. My first instinct is to be under water but I don't knowing mom is seated by the pond painting.

I hear a scream, mom's them Leilani's then a few moments of silence before I hear heavy footsteps of people running towards the pond.

I quickly swim out of the pond, rushing towards the bank where I had left mom sitting.

The royal guards are everywhere, a lot of talking and confusion. I look to where mom was seated and see a lot of blood, then I see her body laying on the grass. Fuck.

I start running towards her when guards try to stop me. I don't think of my actions because my mother is bleeding, I throw the guard holding me back over my shoulder with the strength I have been told to hide and run towards her.

I can't see straight, maybe it's due to the tears in my eyes but I will think about that later. I pull her body towards my lap, wanting to heal her when I see the single shot that was taken. A clear shot, straight between her eyes. Fuck!!!!!.

I hold her body close, trying to contain the anger that is quickly rising in my body.

Someone tries to guide me to my room where they think it is safe but I just want to stay here with my mom. I hadn't I learned to heal, not that is would work but fuck. My anger starts to get the better of me, I can feel it, I can feel the change in me.

My fingers start to change first, I feel my nails lengthen and strengthen. I am angry, mad and sad, all emotions that I can't control at the moment and I know I am about to transform.

I feel a short sharp pain at the back of my head then everything goes black.

I wake up later on a soft place and I blink trying to figure out where I am.

My head hurts like a bitch though, who the fuck hit me behind my head. I hear footsteps approaching the room I am in when it all comes back to me. Mom. Gareth. Leilani. Fuck

The door to my bedroom is opened and father steps in looking worse for wear. His eyes are rimmed red, his royal gown with stains of blood which means he was in a meeting when he had been told about the attack.

He takes a seat beside me and pulls me into a hug. I know then that the situation can not be reversed, mom is gone.
I cry, letting all my emotions out and father holds me.
I scream and scratch and kick and he just holds me. When a gifted let's his emotions get the better of him, the consequences can be dire so I let it all out.
We stay like that, father and I till I get exhausted and fall asleep.
I wake up to sunlight streaming through my windows, I have a fresh change of clothes on and there's a tray of breakfast waiting for me. I go and use the bathroom then come to eat. I want to say I feel something but I don't, I feel numb. It's like all my feelings were drained out of me. One thing I do feel though is guilt, guilt that I talked to Gareth that way on our way to the gardens even though he was only trying to protect me. Guilt that I hadn't learnt to heal because maybe if I had learnt to heal, I would have saved mom. Guilt that I didn't know shit about Leilani or Gareth despite them being constant in my life since the day I was born. Guilt is all I feel and nothing else.
The scrambled eggs I am chewing taste more like sand and less like eggs but I just swallow them because even I am intelligent enough to know I need to eat.
I turn the tv in my room and I see the media standing a good distance away from the palace trying to get pictures of the newly widowed and orphan pair. Fucking vultures is what they are, the media are fucking vultures who will take apart and chew anything left if me.
I change the channel and I find out that all the channels in Ambrosia are all covering the death of mom. I throw away the remote and lay on my back trying to sleep but I know that the sleep I have managed to get yesterday is all I am ever going to get for a long time to come.
My bedroom door opens and father walks in.
" Good morning Edward, how did you sleep?" I sit up,
" Good morning father." Is all I say because what is really good about the fucking morning.
" I don't know what to say to Edward except that I am sorry.

Elspeth didn't deserve the end she got and I hope you don't blame yourself for it."

I want to cry but I keep it in because I know that the only reason I got to cry yesterday was because mom had just died. Royals don't cry because it's a sign of weakness.

" How did the attackers get in?" I ask him.

The castle is like a fortress, security everywhere, no one can go in or out without being seen.

" I don't know son, the head of security is looking at security footage from yesterday." He tells me. His voice is resigned and sad.

I have never seen father like this.

" Did they manage to get away?" I ask him instead.

" Yes unfortunately but that's not why I am here. Under normal circumstances, the death of a royal takes time to be mourned but security was breached endangering you, we are going to have your mother's burial tomorrow. Everything has been arranged, the kings and queens of the other kingdoms wanted to make an appearance but I refused it. It will be a small ceremony with just us and a few guards."

He doesn't say anything else but I know what is expected of me. I know the media will be there covering the whole thing, but at least those eyes are eyes that I can't see or feel because they will be in their different home behind their screens and mourning the death of their queen. Father leaves and I am once again left with my thoughts and guilt.

The royal guards are mourning today, a day before mom's burial. They lost not one but two trusted and experienced guards. There's a cemetery outside the castle gate that is reserved for the burial of all royal guards. No one is attending it though because father forbade it and all the royal guards are in a state of panic.

If an assassin can manage to enter and kill the queen and two of their own minus them knowing then they are slacking in their duties.

I wear a hoodie and sweats, concentrate and get a hold of my gift of invisibility and quietly leave my room. I sneak out of the castle yard and go to the royal guard cemetery. It's raining today, a fitting weather for such a shitty day. There's no one at the burial site but the six guards carrying and burying the bodies. No family members though I am not surprised because Garreth was the most private person I ever met. I sit behind the trees and watch as they lower the caskets and bury them.

I cry then because Gareth was like a second father to me despite my bratty behaviour sometimes. I cry because Leilani was the only friend mom had who she was happy and comfortable with. I cry because their killers are still out there somewhere and because there is no one here to mourn them.

It's like they are not important, just another inconvenience to be rid of. The guards bury them and quickly head back to the castle leaving me alone, not that they know I am here. Not even a flower is left there.

I sit in the cemetery till my ass becomes numb and my fingers and hands are white due to the cold before I decide to leave and go back to the castle. Before doing so, I head over to the burial sites to pay my last respects.

I wake up earlier than usual the following morning although I honestly don't think I slept at all last night. I had a nightmare, a terrible one and I know I screamed because I woke screaming with my body covered in sweat. Which was when I decided I wasn't going to sleep at all but watch the moon through my sky light.

It had been a beautiful night, full moon and no clouds with all

the stars out there shining and twinkling.
Mom would have loved it, she would have got her canvas and decided to paint it forgoing sleep all together.
The bids are outside chirping and singing and there is a clear blue sky. I want the birds to drop and die, I want everyone to be as miserable as me but today is serving as a reminder once again that while other people mourn, others celebrate.
I take a shower and have breakfast and wait for the dreaded knock to come.
When the knock comes, I leave my room and go with my guards who have some while quadru8in number. They bow and greet me, none of them offering me any condolences for fear they might speak out of term. I find father and his entourage in the garden and I notice he has also tripled his security.
I greet him quietly and we start walking towards the royal cemetery. This one is reserved for only the members of the royal family. Not many burials have been made here, most of the graves are empty, the ones my father had out there after his supposed deaths over the years. There are a few media people here, all with sympathetic smiles and looks on their faces but I can read their thoughts and their thoughts are anything but.
They are all here with greed and glory in kind, the few invited to attend the funeral of the late queen.
Of all the few people in attendance, only one person feels genuinely sorry, the rest are just here for show and to see what they can get from attending the royal funeral.
Fuck them all.
Mom deserved better than this but I don't Express those feelings, I instead keep my head held down through the whole ceremony and say nothing. I try to make my face look the perfect amount of hurt and not to cry too much.
It is time for the body viewing and I stand and walk behind father. I reach the casket and look at mom one last time. She looks peaceful, still beautiful and lovely. Her hair was combed by someone I guess. I smell a faint trace of her favourite perfume, it smells of roses and a fresh summer afternoon. It's almost like

she's asleep but the bandage around her head, hiding the bullet wound, is a reminder that she is gone. I swear on her grave.

I am not sure how long I stand and stare at her one last time before I feel father put his hand on my shoulder and only then do I see that my nails started to change again.

I quickly walk away,my heart cloudy and black.

I go to stand beside father as they lower her casket in the ground and a part of me goes with her. I know I will never be the same again after this.

I swear right there and then that mom's death. Gareth and Leilani's death will not be in vain. I will God who ever killed them and make them pay if it is the last thing I do.

Chapter 2

Edward Vaughn

It has been two weeks since mom's death and for the most part everything is back to normal I guess. I haven't been to school though and I haven't gone out in a while.

The only things I do are dinners with father each night. I learnt the gift of healing though. A little ironic considering the one time I would have used it I couldn't use it.

My security is still very tight and they still haven't managed to find the assassins. I got a new royal guard from the top five to be in charge of my security.

My busts of emotion and unknowingly starting to transform are now under control so I guess that's nice. I stopped talking much though, I just don't want to I guess.

All the true royal guards are now dead since Gareth was the last to go and I find that still hard to believe sometimes. Everytime I am doing something I am not supposed to be doing,I expect to find Gareth at the next corner lurking or to fly towards me from the crowds above so fast that no one sees him and those who used to see him always thought it was some large bird.

I laugh to myself at that though. I remember telling him once that some kids at school had seen a huge bird fly by the same time he came to stop me from fighting some kid at school who thought I was too pussy to beat him.

I would have thought and I don't think the kid would have survived the fight.

I am in my room sitting by window painting when someone knocks on my door.
" Come in." Donovan walks in and bows to his waist,
" Good afternoon, your highness. Your father requests your presence in his chambers." He continues kneeling despite delivering his message.
" Did he ask you to wait for me?" I ask him getting a little pissed with him waiting for me,
" No, your highness." He responds standing up,
" Then leave. I can find my way to his chambers." I say dismissing him. He leaves and I change my shirt before going to see father.

" You wanted to see me father?" I ask father. He is in his chambers with Conrad the royal adviser.
Conrad is a seventy-nine year old man or at least he is that age to all mortals. He is actually one hundred and fifty years old though. A man so wise beyond his age, his black skin barely showing the signs of aging at all.
" I did, have a seat." Father answers me and I take the seats in front of his desk.
I wait patiently for him to finish writing before he addresses me again.
" There is a school in Quewest, a lovely and secure school in the mountains there." He looks at me expectantly as he speaks.
" And?" I ask him a little confused.
" You will be attending the school. It is safer for you and I don't want to risk your safety."
He stands up and walks to stand by the window.
" I am afraid I don't understand father, I am safe here ain't I. Besides nothing can kill me unless I choose to die so why do I have to go to Quewest?"
I ask him. I have never, not once in my life questioned my father

but today I do that.
" Edward, you are no longer safe here. Yes nothing can kill you but what exactly do we tell the people and the media when you survive attacks and attacks and attacks. Just because they are mortal doesn't mean they are stupid."
He doesn't raise his voice once but I can tell he is upset. Conrad just sits on the other side of the room,a silent observer.
" But father, it still doesn't make any sense. I will be safe like I have always been. The attack on mom won't happen again especially now that we are ready and are expecting attacks like that."
I sound desperate at the moment I know and that's because I am. I just lost one parent and I am not willing or ready to lose another.
" Edward, the attack on your mother wasn't just random. It was targeted and the bullet she took was meant for you." His words are like a punch in the gut.
" WHAT." He says nothing just takes the form I found him signing and hands it to me.
" You leave in two days, Edward. Don't make me repeat myself."
Fuck.

Quewest is the smallest of the four kingdoms, the most mountainous and the one kingdom anyone who wants to be forgotten goes. I guess I now fall in the forgotten category.
My mind is a jungle of thoughts as the plane starts to land. The assassins had been after me. That makes no sense though especially since i can't exactly be killed not that they know that. Their stupidity and ignorance cost me the death of my mother and one of my friends.
The flight attendant tells us to fasten our seatbelts and I breathe in a little, counting to ten because despite my immortality and

lack of getting hurt. I still have fears.

After we land, there's a small army of servants and maybe a dozen black cars parked at the airport waiting for my arrival. If I had gone to any other kingdom I would have drawn attention to myself but in Quewest, the rich are always coming to stay so it's normal.

Father wasn't joking when he said he wanted to protect me or hide me is what I would say.

The mountains of Que are shining, the snow sparkling against the rays of the sun.

I am not sure how long the drive to my new 'home' takes. It isn't until a guard opens my door that I realize we have arrived.

The house father bought is nestled in a canopy of trees, hidden from prying eyes. It has been built to blend in with the rest of the mountains so you wouldn't know it even existed unless someone told you it did.

A woman comes out of the house introducing herself as the housekeeper and I don't pay her any attention.

She takes me on a tour which I don't finish because the moment she opens the door to my bedroom, I lock the door in her face. Mom would have been pissed and asked me to apologise despite being a prince and I would have done it but lucky for me I have no parents controlling me.

I prepare a bath to soak my sore muscles because I had a long flight. It only occurs to me while I am in the tub that I haven't spoken a single word since morning.

I would never tell father this but I have been enjoying living in the Que mountains. At Least I was until I received an order to start attending the classes I had been skipping. I never even started attending the fucking school here and none of the servants or guards are willing to cross paths with me because I

apparently have a temper that has got quite a reputation for me. Father won't call or come to check on me himself for fear of being traced and whoever hired the assassins finding me which is something he doesn't want.
So he has taken to sending me letters. Really long fucking letters with threat that I am bit willing to see come to pass so I am been a good little boy and starting school the coming week.
I am in my room at the moment trying to find inspiration, trying to paint something as a way to get closer to mom or the memory of her. I haven't been able to paint shit since her death and I have been trying because painting and afternoon tea were the only activities we did together.
Despite been in the woods ina house at the bottom of the mountain, you would expect the fucking place to be quite as a morgue but fuck no it isn't.
The guards outside my door are thinking of one of the maids named Betty and how she has a tight little ass. Fucking assholes. I shit off my thoughts once more, get a blank canvas and start painting.
I open my imagination, lock away all my thoughts and decide to let the mind and hands do all the work.
I don't get a fucking drop of inspiration and it's like my art just went away. Fuck. I grab the canvas and throw it against the wall. Fuck!!!!! I want to feel something, I want to cry or shout or scream at the top of my fucking lungs but I do non of those things. I instead go out for a walk because even in my sleep my guilt follows and wont let me be. Well at least I have school to fucking look forward to.

Que high school is the most overpriced and private school in the whole of Quewest hell, maybe even in all the four kingdoms. The fact that is it the most expensive school shows in terms of security and NDAs signed at the fucking school. Which would explain why father chose this school in particular. He still has his trust issues though and that shows because three of my guards are posing as teachers around the school.

I arrived late because I didn't want to come but I had to because well father was summoned and he always gets what he wants. The principal is an ass kisser and if her whole call me anytime you need help didn't tell me that already her thoughts drew the whole fucking picture out for me. She escorts me to class because either her duty and honor or some bullshit like before I tune her out, thoughts and all.

The class she takes to is noisy. I can hear all their thoughts as she introduces me.

The pity, the money hungry ones, the fame chasers, the people pleasers all of them. I quickly take a seat at the back of the class and try to tune all their thoughts out but it proves difficult when I can now feel eyes on me. Fuck. Today is going to be the longest day ever.

I somehow manage to survive a week at Que, though it has taken little for me not to lose my shit and patience.

After a week of being pestered and talked to, the other students finally got the message I am not interested in making friends because they stopped trying to talk to me.

I am looking for a table to sit at and read a book during lunch when I spot one in a hidden corner. I quickly sit there and roll my eyes a little when I see one if my guards try and fail to secretly sit a few feet away from me.

" Aren't your security supposed to be a secret or something? Whatever that guy is doing isn't secretive."

A voice beside me says. I didn't even hear the person take a seat beside me but he has to have some balls to sit next to me.

I turn to look at the owner of the voice and find a teenage boy, probably my age.
His brown hair is greasy which means he hasn't washed it in weeks which I find weird because all the boys my age here probably take hours in a shower trying to get the perfect hairstyle.
Then the most refreshing thing happens, I read his thoughts and I am shocked. His mind is completely occupied with science and some papers he has due in an hour. He thinks about how he has to help his younger sister with some homework and I quickly stop myself from reading some more.
" Sorry, forgot I was talking to you. Rumor has it you only say five words in a day."
It's only after he says this that u realize that I just have spaced out. My face must look shocked because she quickly adds,
" Don't worry. The others don't pay much attention to the teachers so I don't think they noticed him."
I actually forgot we where talking about my security. He ignores me after imparting his words of wisdom and starts to eat.
I look at his food and internally throw up because what the fuck is he eating.
His banana must have seen better days and I swear I can see the mold on his bread. I don't ask him anything about it though, I just watch as he eats it like it is the most amazing meal he has ever had.
Once he is done with his lunch,he cleans up and is about to stand when I stretch my hand out as a way of greeting. He looks at me weirdly before weirdly shaking my hand,
" Edward." I tell him.
He laughs at me like I just said the most funny thing he has ever heard,
" I know dude. Who doesn't know you in the whole school. Marshall." He tells me before leaving me alone.
I was content with being alone all the time but maybe having a companion isn't so hard. I signal for my not so secret guard to come to me. When he is within hearing distance I tell him to find

out everything he can about Marshall.

∞∞∞

Marshall Thatcher is fifteen years old. He is the first child in a family of two, his younger sister is nine years old and his father died some years ago. His mother is slowly dying from a wasting disease and the reason he learns at Que is because of a scholarship he got two years ago.

The guy's a genius in math.

He works part time to take care of his mother and sister.

It's amazing the amount of information you can have access to when you are rich.

During lunch today, I go and sit in the same corner like yesterday and wait. Just like yesterday he comes and takes a seat beside me. The only difference today is the fact that I was expecting him.

" Good afternoon Edward." He greets me. He doesn't expect or wait for me to answer him which suits me just fine. Today his lunch is what appears to have been an apple in another lifetime. The poor fruit doesn't have a normal color if a fruit but is instead brown in color.

I push a plate of the food my cook prepared in front of him. I can already hear his objections on his mind before he says them and I am prepared,

" My cook prepared too much. Take it." His objections die because apparently I don't speak. He accepts the food and today he doesn't leave just after he is done with his lunch. He instead stays and studies while I read my book. I feel like a five year old learning how to make friends again but at least this time I don't have other kids' thoughts screaming in my head.

My little ritual with Marshall continues for about two weeks. Father found out about it, was about to have Marshall transferred to another school because Lord knows I can't make a friend but then he let go when the teachers around said it was good me for to interact with at least one person in school. Not that I cared.

" You are really bad at science." Marshall says while we have lunch in our little corner. Weird I know. Truth is I am very good at science but I noticed that he eats a quarter of the food I give him then packs the rest up. Leaving me to believe that he takes the rest home to his mother and sister. So I decided what the heck, a few bad grades and I can hire him as my tutor because Marshall will never accept a handout. The only reason he eats lunch with me is because I tell him I don't like to waste food.

" Yeah, I need a tutor, you." He looks at me, considering the offer. One thing we have also come to an understanding of is the fact that I just won't talk if I don't want to. After a few days of attempting to start random conversations with me, he started holding up all ends of the conversations we have. So the fact that I asked him is a big deal for him I guess especially if his thoughts are any giveaway.

I push a check of ten thousands in front of him.

He chokes on his juice when he sees the amount of money on the check.

" Edward, bro I appreciate the sentiment but this is too much for a tutor. I can't accept it." He starts pushing it back to me but I don't let him. I fold the check and put it in his pocket.

" It's a lot of money, yes but then, when you tutor me, I will be the only person you work for. No one gets to know you work for the royal family and you sign a NDA. Hence the reason it's a lot or too much."

Truth is,I thought ten thousand wasn't enough when I first thought of this. I mean father has to send me millions for just a month's expenses and I don't even pay any of the servants or guards.

" Wow, Edward... I don't know what to say. Thank you so much."
I turn around, a little uncomfortable at the show of affection.
I have never met a person like Marshall before because I thought all mortals are conceited and self centred. But at a young age he has to shoulder too much which I am sure is suffocating for him sometimes.
" When do you want us to make a schedule so I can know when to work?" He asks, his eyes a little red from crying I think. I am not very good with other people's emotions.
" My driver will drive you to my house after school, don't be late." I tell him before leaving. I promised I would go to school. I didn't say anything about staying in school till classes were over. The only reason I stay till lunch is because I have to give Marshall food, I doubt if he even notices that I never eat.
I am in my gym, working out when someone knocks on my door. No one comes to disturb me which means Marshall is here. I wear a shirt before opening the door.
" I mean I know that the royal family of Ambrosia is rich but this house is like a fuck you to all the elite of Quewest." He tells me, smiling. I close the door behind him as he walks around the room looking at my equipment and what not.
" You should have seen the kids at school when they saw me enter your car, they all probably think you're gay because I am literally the only person you talk to at school or at least your version if talking." What the fuck. I am not gay, I mean I have never slept with a girl before but I know I am straight, I like women.
" Wait you're not gay are you?" He asks me as if it's just now occurring to him that I might be.
" Fuck you." He smirks,
" Edward, such language is not becoming of a prince." I laugh a little,something I haven't done in a long time.
" Seriously dude, you have a potty mouth on you." I ignore him as I look for another pair of sweatpants. I find a new black pair I haven't worn yet and give them to him with a pair of workout shoes.

" The changing room is the first door on your left." I tell him.
He goes to change without asking me any questions. When he comes back,I hand him boxing gloves.
" I am not much of a fighter." Is all he tells me.
" No shit Sherlock, just get the gloves and take a hit at me."
I have seen him get beaten so many fucking times at school I am shocked he still had all his bones working. The shots of bullying and beating him stopped after we started hanging out but I know that the moment you leave school, they beat the shit out of him. Evidence of their beatings can be seen right now since I didn't give him a shirt, his skin is purple and blue in some areas, swollen and untreated.
He takes a hit at me which I manage to block. He tries to take another one and I block him again before he finds himself on his ass.
" Edward, I don't think this is part of tutoring." He is breathing hard after two hits and I am sure his arse will be a pain to sit on for the next few days.
" Get up, take a hit at me."
I help him stand up and he tries to take a cheap shot at me. I block him and he ends up on his ass again.
This time he doesn't stay down though, he gets up and tries again. He didn't land a single shot at me today but at least he learnt a few self defense moves.

Marshall has been 'tutoring' for maybe two months and he has learnt to defend himself and fight. I am proud to say that no one at school bullies him anymore.
He spends most of his afternoons at my house, I have never been to his house which is where I am heading at the moment.
He called to cancel his tutor session today because his mother

isn't doing so well today.

I have of course sneaked out of the house to go and see him.

The rood I am taking at the moment is so bad that I doubt if anyone even uses it because it's a fucking death trap.

The houses here are rundown and in such bad conditions that I am surprised they are even standing up. The house I am looking for in the one at the end of the road and the most rundown of them all.

I knock in the door and a little girl opens the door. Mona. She is the exact replica of Marshall only in girl tween girl form. She has brown hair and blue eyes. She first doesn't say anything, just looks at me suspiciously and I stand her inspection. Her thoughts are all curious though and a little sad which I am guessing is due to the mother being sick.

" Come in." She says after some minutes,I walk past her into what appears to be the living room and kitchen and bedroom.

It's hard to believe that there are people living like this while the royal family of Quewest sleeps in their beds made of gold. Are there places like this back in Ambrosia? No I mean if they existed, father must have built better ones for the people that need them right. I make a vow to myself that when I become king, things will be different around Ambrosia.

" Edward, what are you doing here?" Marshall looks tired and his eyes are swollen from lack of sleep.

" I came to see your mother." I don't like to beat around the Bush. Besides, I did come to see his mother.

" She's not in any shape of physical form to see guests at the moment." I just now notice there's a curtain as some form of privacy for whoever is behind it.

" My house keeper sent some medicine." Marshall and my house keeper have formed some sort of relationship. She loves to feed him whenever he comes home and packs so much food for him that he could feed an entire army if he wanted to. I know he won't say no to her. I just need a few moments alone with his mother.

" Fine but be quick,she needs to rest."

We go behind the curtain and see a slight figure sleeping. I can hear her wheeze from where I stand and I am shocked she's managed to survive this long. I sit on the chair next to the bed and hold her hand. She opens her eyes and looks at me,
" Mom, this is Edward, the prince I told you about." Her eyes widen, her thoughts are all for her children though. What will happen to them if she dies and what not.
" I am his friend, Edward, yes." Marshall rolls his eyes at me.
" Marshall, can I get a glass of water." He looks reluctant to leave but his mother urges him to go and he does. I can feel the pain this woman is in and it is overpowering, I know I can heal myself but what this mortal is going through is painful.
I hold her small hand in both of mine. I know father would probably kill me if he finds out what I want to do but I won't let my friend lose his mother because I know what that feels like and I wouldn't wish such a feeling even on my worst enemy.
I reach deep within myself and summon all the power and energy I can, I feel a little tingling and I know my hands have the glow of a night fly when I hear Marshall's mother gasp softly. She says nothing though and I continue because I don't want Marshall to see me doing this. I take all her pain away and heal her, I take it all and shoulder it as my own and my breaths become shallow due to the pain.
When u finally let go of her hand and open my eyes she quickly covers them with the hand I had been holding.
Fuck. My eyes must have changed during the healing. I breath in and try to change them back because it's going to be hard to explain to her son how my blue eyes are low red.
When I open my eyes after a few seconds she smiles at me. She looks better now and I know she's okay. It will take time for her to be back to normal, for her to gain back all her lost weight and her natural color but at least she's now okay.
" I have heard of you, I thought it was just an old maids tail but you are real." He tells me, wonder evident in her voice.
" Please don't tell your son." I ask her. A big ask I know.
" I will take this to my grave, your highness. You have given me

another chance at life. Thank you."

I believe her and I know she speaks the truth.

A little uncomfortable with all the praise, I get up about to leave.

" Your highness, thank you not just for me but my son as well. He seems lighter these last few months, not worried. My family is forever in your debt." I nod and leave, closing the curtains behind me.

" Didn't you want water Edward?" Marshall asks me but I ignore him and just get the hell out of the house. Fuck.

What if the healing hadn't worked but instead killed her faster like the roses. Fuck fuck fuck.

Marshall shows up for tutoring the next day. He feels lighter, like a great burden has been lifted off his shoulders. We don't learn though, my housekeeper feeds him till he is sure he is going to explode then he falls asleep on the couch in my study.

His mother is doing well thanks to the 'medicine' our housekeeper sent and she was up and about today. Despite my worries and concern, hearing that makes me happy and I am glad I did what I did.

Chapter 3

Edward Vaughn
Fifteen Years Later

" You are expected to come back to Ambrosia next week." Father says. We have been on a video call for the last fifteen minutes which is a record because the last fifteen minutes have gone by emails and letters. So imagine my shock when he summons me back.

I haven't been in Ambrosia since leaving for school. I like to call it my father protecting me while the media loves to call it me being punished because why else would a grieving man send his child to a school in an unknown location.

I didn't even attend his wedding to my stepmother which just seemed to heighten the rumours being spread by the press.

I just didn't want to go home yet and I am honestly not ready but when father summons you go.

He ends the call and I sigh. Fuck. I have been travelling around the four kingdoms since the day I turned twenty-two. I am not exactly the bad boy but I do have a reputation I guess.

Marshall is the one who made most of the headlines though, bad boy billionaire seen on watch having a foursome or some shit. I am the quiet one of the two of us. The level headed one.

Not all their headlines are true though but we just let them run with it.

" Is it that bad?" Marshall asks me. He has a system of entering my room without knocking. I asked him to knock and all he said

was it's not like I will find fucking or something.
" He wants me back in Ambrose by next week." His eyes widen and he whistles,
" That bad huh. Well then, we are travelling to Ambrosia next week. Lord knows I have been wanting to see it." I roll my eyes as my inner self goes on a battle .
Ambrosia has so many of my demons locked up and I know going back will be opening a wound. But then it's not like I can rule while living in Quewest. Fuck.
" Edward, you will be fine, trust me." Of course he thinks that I will be fine, he always has faith in me even during the most stupid situations and the problem is his thoughts are always matching his words. He never lies to me so even now I know he believe that I will be okay but I know myself,this fucking visit won't end well.
" Come on now, go and shower because mom wants to cook us dinner." Well at least that can cheer me up. Marley loves to cook for us.

∞∞∞

" Come on boys, eat up. I spent three hours on this meal." Marley tells us as she puts more food on my plate.
Looking at her now, anyone who knew her then would be shocked she survived but she did.
We developed a sort of understanding between us since the day I healed, she didn't tell anyone what happened true to her word. She kind of adopted me and claimed me as her own. She doesn't seem bothered by my silence much and I can go as far as to say she loves me.
Marshall's whole family welcomed and embraced me like I was one of them and I am forever grateful for that.
" We are travelling to Ambrosia next week." Marshall says casually. Marley's spoon stops halfway to her mouth, her eyes

widening slightly.
" I didn't know you were planning on going back Edward. Is everything okay." She directs the question to Marshall even though she is talking to me.
" Everything is fine mom, the king just summoned him back and I decided to go with him." He says.
" That and I am going to get married in three months." I tell them.
Marshall chokes on his wine and Marley looks a little pale. Ah fuck.
" I didn't know you had been seen someone, Edward." Marley says and I swallow, my throat suddenly dry.
" I am not, it's an arranged marriage but it's yet to be confirmed." I tell them and that's all I am willing to share at the moment.
" When were you playing on telling me this? Dude, marriage is a huge deal and you didn't even think to tell me." I sigh. Marshall acts like a woman(no offense) with his emotions all over the place.
" He has told you now he hasn't, now eat up." It's not a request and Marshall doesn't bring my marriage up for the rest of the evening.
Marley leaves after dinner and Marshall escorts her out. I go to my room to take a shower because fuck today has been one hell of a day.
I am washing my hair when I hear Marshall enter my room.
" Marriage really, Edward. You don't have to do it, you know, you don't have to go back. You don't need his fucking money because we have made plenty of our own."
I mean he's not wrong. We started a company, one public under our real names and a private research lab for Marshall under fake names. They are both doing well and I am fucking rich, my great great grandchildren can leave in luxury.
I am going back to Ambrosia, I will marry whoever it is father has arranged for me to marry and I will rule Ambrosia when he abdicates. I want to do this so it's not that easy.
" I want to do this Marshall. I am going back to Ambrosia next

week, you can come along if you want but I am leaving on Sunday afternoon with or without you." I tell him.
I hear him leave and bang the door on his way out.
I take a few deep breaths trying to calm myself, leaning against the shower wall. Well then, Ambrosia here I come.

Ambrosia, like all the kingdoms, is a beautiful sight in the evenings. The skyscrapers with their lights on, twinkling against the skyline as my jet descends and starts to land.
Marshall snores softly in the seat next to mine, he fell asleep the second the plane ascended. I tried to sleep but I couldn't, my stomach is tied in so many knots I am afraid I might get indigestion. The pilot informs me of the landing and I close my eyes trying to calm my nerves.
We land and I am the first person who disembarks.
There's a lot if security and a few royal guards. I see Conrad and smile a little. My father's royal adviser hasn't aged since the last time I saw him.
" Welcome home, your highness." He says, bowing slightly. I raise my hand signalling him to stand up.
" Well damn." Marshall says behind me.
" Well home Mr Thatcher." Conrad tells Marshall who nods to him absent mindedly.
" Your father is very pleased with your return, your highness and he can't wait to see you tomorrow. Well, we best be on my way, Donovan and the other royal guards have taken extra measures to ensure your safety so please abide by them. Until we meet again, your highness." He bows again before leaving, two guards escorting him.
" Welcome home your highness." Donovan says, bowing to his waist. He has grown a bit and he thinks the same of me, his thoughts screaming at me. He has been promoted and since

takenGarett's position as main royal guard. I raise my hand, telling him to stand up.

" I trust you had a pleasant flight." He says.

I nod my head once and he stops talking.

A woman with black hair, scratch that, a young woman with black hair comes and stands next to him.

" Welcome home your highness." She greets, bowing as well. I raise my hand and she stands up. She is a very beautiful woman and I don't use this word lightly. She is probably five feet and 6 inches with hazel eyes. She also looks young. My best guess is she is maybe twenty years old.

She's wearing a very small dress and I use the term loosely because the scrap of fabric she is wearing barely covers anything.

I open my mind to the thoughts of the other royal guards and herself because I am confused as fuck. Her thoughts are all about how she respects me, the other royal guards all have the same sentiment except it is directed at her. I can tell immediately that she is respected by her peers.

From Donovan though, he is very upset and now I am intrigued and I can't wait to find out who this lovely lady is.

" This is Leilani Adair, your highness, your personal royal guard." Donacan says,but I don't pay much attention.

My mind frozen.

Leilani.

" Leinani, are you related to the late Leilani?" I ask her, the first words I have spoken since arriving.

" The Leilani, it would have been an honor to be related to such a great woman but I am afraid we just share the same name." She says with a smile.

I look at her for a long time till she starts to blush before I come out of my daze. She looks a little uncomfortable and I honestly don't blame.

" Anyway, she will be posing as you mistress until we know you will be safe." A Lot of questions come to mind.

Why do I need her pretending is one of the first ones really. Why would father ask me to come back if the situation here was really that dire that I needed to a royal guard pretending to date and to live with me.

" We wanted to reduce your security but we also didn't want to leave you vulnerable. So we came up with this plan. Leilani is the best royal guard there is so you will be safe with her."

Well at least he thought of something.

Adair looks around the airport,to everyone around, she is simply bored but to someone with a trained eye she is scanning the place, checking for anything out of place.

All the other guards are doing it; she is just more discreet than them. I read Donovan's mind once more and I almost laugh to myself.

I am not sure of the relationship that he and Adair share but he is not pleased with his own plan one bit. Which brings so many questions like why did he agree to it in the first place but I don't ask any questions.

I make sure to keep my face blank and devoid of any emotions.

" Is that all or did you plan on making me spend the night at the airport?" I ask Donovan and he flushes, looking quite uncomfortable.

" I am so sorry, your highness. Right this way." He says turning around and guiding us to one of the waiting cars.

Adair walks beside me, a little too close for my comfort but I don't say anything.

" Well shit, if I had known this was how your coming back to Ambrosia would.have gone,I would have dragged you back myself just for the entertainment." Marshall says behind me and I almost jump out of my skin.

Fucking Marshall, I forgot he was even there the moment I saw Adair.

" Shut the fuck up."

I tell him between clenched teeth. He throws his head back and laughs, Adair looks at him curiously but says nothing. One of the guards opens the door for us and we all get in. I am still trying to wrap my head around the whole mistress bodyguard thing.

The car feels so bloody small considering it's a stretch limo. Adair sits on one side and Marshall sits next to me, his eyes looking at the sites as we pass. His mind is filled with nothing but appreciation and my chest fills with pride.
Maybe I came back home against my will and due to my father's summons but I am proud to say that I will one day rule Ambrosia. The kingdom of Ambrosia is one of the greatest and richest kingdoms and I am happy to say I will be part of its even greater future.

Twenty-one is a big deal for everyone and it is even an even bigger deal in my family. I am not sure who started the tradition but every twenty-first birthday, a prince of Ambrosia is given a piece of land or in my case quarter of the kingdom, papers signed and everything.
I built a 'house' when I turned twenty-one because as much as I loved the castle I didn't want to be in there for longer than necessary.
When I had the house built, I valued my privacy above all else so the house sits in the middle of a small forest.
Nothing wild but it is just in the midst of nature because I feel at one with nature, my gifts are always most powerful when I am one with nature so it is a win-win situation.
When we reach the driveway, I come out of the car to admire the house because wow.
" Damn, you did good Edward, you did good."
Marshall says coming to stand besides me. I had a vision for the house and the builders brought that vision to life.
Servants and guards come out of the house to greet and welcome me home, bowing and what not but I dismiss them because it has been a long day and all I want to do is rest.
I head straight to my room to take a shower not bothering to

show Marshall around because he can find his own way.
I am about to enter my room when I see Adair going into the room next to mine, my art room. I haven't been able to draw since the death of mom but I guess I still carry hope that I will be able to paint and draw again so I had the builder make this room for that exact reason.
" Did you need something?" I ask her because I am genuinely curious,
" Nope. This is my room for the duration of our???" She stops talking for a while as if trying to find the right words to use,
" I want to say relationship but I think that's too strong a word but anyway I will be sleeping in this room until further notice I guess. Good night, your highness." She says before entering the room and closing the door behind her. Fuck.

I have just finished taking my shower and have a towel wrapped around my waist when Marshall enters my room without knocking. Some maids come in after him carrying trays of food. I ignore them all and continue getting ready for bed. I grab my sweat pants and drop my towel so I can wear them when one of the maids screams.
I turn around, my eyes scanning her for any injuries or signs of danger but she doesn't seem to be bleeding which is a good sign. Why the fuck is she sreaming though. The door opens and Adair walks in at a slow pace wearing a very short, silky dress with her hair down.
" Wear your fucking pants or she won't stop screaming her fucking head off." Marshall says from the corner of the room. Fuck I forgot he was here.
I wear my sweats as Adair asks the maids to leave. I am very comfortable in my nakedness but I now feel uncomfortable.
" Not that it's my place to say anything, your highness, but next

time try to be a little more dressed in front of the maids. Enjoy your meal." She quickly leaves, closing the door behind.
" Damn. I am not complaining about seen your balls because I have seen them so many fucking times I would be worried if you didn't show them to me every once in a while but I don't think she was impressed."
Marshall says with a mouth full of food. How do I keep on forgetting he is in the room?
" Haha, very funny. Now please leave, I need to sleep because I have a long week ahead of me." I tell him grabbing a scone from the tray of food the maids brought in. I don't wait for him to say anything before leaving and going out to the balcony.
I sit outside and just relax. No one, no intruding thoughts just me looking at the trees and stars.
I feel like someone is watching me after some time but there is no one out but me. I open my mind and try to find the person's thoughts but when I feel nothing I ignore the feeling and go inside.

Chapter 4

Edward Vaughn

I am running or at least I am trying to but I keep on falling. Someone is chasing me, I can't see their face, not that I have ever been able to see them. I am running through a forest, and I feel a great deal of pain, my heart blackened by all the pain and sorrow.

After falling for the fourth time I realise I am dreaming and try to wake up but it's like I am part of the dream and the dream won't let me go. I try to wake up but it's like something keeps on pulling me back in. I struggle with the thing holding me back in my dream before I am finally able to wake up.

I am sweaty and my heart is beating so fast. My sheets are half wet and damp from my sweat. Fuck.

I haven't had a nightmare in a long time but this one felt more real like it had been happening. I sit up and check the time on my watch. 4AM. Right on time I guess.

I get a towel and change my sweats before going to the home gym to work out. I have a few more hours before Marshall or anyone else wakes up.

I stop in my tracks when I find Adair working out. I am not used to other people being awake this early in the morning with me but I don't say a word. She's wearing very little shorts and an even smaller shirt that leaves nothing to my imagination. I quickly turn around and put my towel down before my body starts acting with a mind of its own.

" Good morning, Your highness." I turn around and find she has bowed in greeting and for the first time in my life I feel uncomfortable at being greeted in such a fashion.
" Good morning Adair. Please stand up, you don't have to greet me in such a fashion every time you see me you know." She smiles sheepishly,
" Well now I do." And she goes back to her workout.
I ignore her as best as I can during my workout although I end up working out more than I usually do because I don't want to leave before her, especially since I found her and she works out for three hours,leaving the gym at 6AM.
I know I can heal and the pain I feel in my legs can easily go away but what the fuck do these people eat. She walked out of the gym like it was nothing but I saw her work out routine and I can honestly say it isn't for the weak.
I go to my room and shower before heading downstairs for breakfast with Marshall.
We have a little ritual, no matter how busy our days are or where we had been the night before. We always meet every morning for breakfast, he talks and I listen and sometimes I say a word or two but mostly he talks. I have a very busy day today, I have to meet father at the palace, some ass kissing ministers then meetings for the whole day.
I know I will be tired to the bone at the end especially considering the start I had.
They say joy comes in the morning but if my dream had been any indication, I was going to have a shitty day.
I find Marshall and Adair having breakfast, the only two people in the dining room. They are talking and laughing like they are old friends, which isn't surprising because Marshall is a social butterfly. He will blend into any environment.
I give him a little head nod as a form of greeting then I grab some toasted bread and scrambled eggs and bacon from the breakfast table set near the window. The food that has been prepared could feed an army and I am itching to tell the cook to prepare little food going forward but I keep my mouth shut. I hate

wasting food, Marshall is the only one who knows this.

I sit at the head of the table and start eating, not saying a word to the conversation I found, just listening. Adair's mind is filled with so many questions, I can feel them all but she keeps them in, trained to not show curiosity. She just listens and laughs at some of Marshall's stories about something Mona did.

" How old are you, if you don't mind me asking that is." Marshall looks uncomfortable after asking his question but I am also genuinely curious to hear Adair's answer so I say nothing, I just sit and listen.

" Oh, I am twenty-two." She says, blushing a little. I choke on my food because fuck.

" How old were you when you joined?" I find myself asking. Marshall seems surprised to hear me talk since well our breakfasts can go on for an hour and I never say anything.

" I started training when I was maybe six, I don't remember the exact age. Learning to fight here and there, I know it sounds weird a six year old learning how to handle a knife but I liked it. When I turned fourteen, my grandma died. I tried out with a fake age, got into the royal guard but then Devon found out my age. I thought he would have me kicked off the team but he let me stay and well here I am." She says a little sheepishly.

I have so many questions but I don't ask any of them because I know that will not look good at all.

" Wow, that's incredible. Even before I met Edward, I always heard about the royal guard of Ambrosia. You guys are legendary throughout all four kingdoms." Marshall tells her.

He is not wrong, if there was ever a war that broke out or a misunderstanding,the royal guard have always been called to handle it because it is what they do.

But to be picked at the age of fourteen tells me all I need to know about Adair, she is a woman not to be messed with.

" While you attend your meetings, I will be taking a tour of Ambrosia so don't worry about me." Marshall tells me standing up.

" I was not worried about you, just don't get killed. Take some security." I tell him.

He nods and leaves, leaving me and Adair in awkward silence.

After a few uncomfortable minutes, Adair stands as well.

" I will meet you outside your highness." She tells me before leaving.

It's only after she leaves the dining room that I notice she is wearing sweatpants and a shirt that looks too big to belong to her that I notice that these are the most clothes I have seen her in since meeting her yesterday.

After breakfast, I change into my royal robes, the official attire of the court of Ambrosia. The robes are blue and purple in color, the official colors of Ambrosia.

A servant had brought in my crown while I had been having my breakfast. I look at it, my feelings mixed. I haven't worn the crown as the crown prince of Ambrosia in over fourteen years. The crown is golden, made from real gold with blue and purple emeralds, the source of wealth of Ambrosia. Fuck.

I put it on my head and stare at my reflection in the mirror. I have my mother's blue eyes and my father's blond hair but that's all I get from either of them.

In the mirror is Edward Vaughn Lennon, the crown prince of Ambrosia and heir to the throne but I feel anything but that.

I leave my room and servants and guards bow all the way paying respect. Until this morning and putting on the crown, the reality of what my life was going to be hadn't really set in but now that it is looking at me right in the face as yet another maid bows,I know I can't ignore it for long.

I find Adair and her security team outside waiting for me with cars waiting.

Adair is back to wearing her ridiculously small dresses that do little to hide what she has. She starts to bow when she sees me but I quickly hold her hands, stopping her because Lord knows what the guards behind her will see because her dress is really short.

I understand the whole mistress ruse but her dresses really have to go. All the guards with her don't seem disturbed her attire and when I read their thoughts, all I feel is genuine respect for her and admiration.

She must really be good at what she does.

A royal guard opens the door for me and I wait for Adair to get in the car before getting in after her.

If I thought her dress was short when she was standing well it gets shorter when she sits and she has me wondering what wrong I did in my past life for me to be tortured like this in my present life.

The drive to the castle isn't long and Adiar says nothing the whole ride there.

When we get to the palace, I need a moment to myself. I want to open my windows and look at it but I can't because that goes against security protocol.

I haven't been home in almost fifteen years and it goes to say that my emotions are all over the place.

I didn't even come for father's wedding, tongues wagged, people had shit to say and the media had a field day with it but I just didn't want to come so father didn't push me to come.

His wife is okay I think. I haven't met her yet and all our conversations last about a minute or so.

I have nothing against Bella. I just don't like to talk, I guess.

" Reginald, stop the car here then take the prince to the court." Adair says breaking my thoughts. Reginald, who I am guessing is the driver, does as he is told and says nothing.

Adair gets out of the car and I can hear them all. The media people outside wanting to take pictures, waiting patiently like vultures wanting to feed on the body of the dead.

Before the guard who opened the door for Adair can close it again, Adair makes a show of leaning back into the car and kissing me goodbye. The kiss is unexpected but not unpleasant.

I hear a few gasps and I know whoever is outside just got a good look at what Ada6has under that little thing she calls a dress.

I hear their thoughts then, the greed,the men wishing it's them who possesses her, the women wishing it was them with me and not her and the indifference from Adair. She smiles at me

and she's gone in the blink of an eye, the car door is closed and Reginald drives away, going to the forbidden parts of the castle, the court.
The kiss or rather peck is a welcome distraction especially with what I have ahead of me.

∞∞∞

The car parks, the inside of the car is quiet because my car is soundproof and bullet proof though I don't need a soundproof car to know that it is quiet outside.
Someone opens the door for me and I take a deep breath before stepping out. I blink a little to adjust to the sunlight and look straight into the ember eyes of my father. He hasn't aged a little. To everyone he looks like a normal sixty-five year old man but I know better.
I bow to him and he grabs my hand to stop me. He smiles and pulls me into a big hug. I breathe a little easier after because I am finally home with my father.
" Welcome home Edward." He says.
" Thank you father. It's good to be back." I tell him, I want to say I mean it but my heart isn't settled. It's now that I notice the ministers and dukes standing outside the court waiting to welcome me. I close my mind up immediately to avoid reading any of their thoughts and I know my day has begun.
I walk behind father as we enter the court, nod to the people bowing and greeting me but say nothing else. We enter court and it's all business after.

∞∞∞

" Join me for a drink." Father says after the last session of court is adjourned. We are the first to leave and Donovan is on our heels

following father.
I noticed him the whole day, lurking and hiding, protecting father not that he needs it.
" I would like to." I answer because I know he wasn't asking me, it was a command albeit a thinly disguised one.
" Good, we have a lot to catch up on." He says to me,
I don't reply, I simply nod and follow him. He is stopped by someone who wants to have a word with him bit I don't wait for him. I go straight to his study and wait for him there.
I have had a long day and my head hurts like a bitch.
Court has never been easy, listening to complaints, rules and arguments, seeing what can be done and what not. I tried to keep my mind blocked but every now and then my shield would drop and all their thoughts would come at me in full speed. The screams of the one suffering silently, the pain that only they can feel, the greed, the anger, the jealousy and in the few instances, the joy.
I walk around father's study alone at least. I see the chair I sat on the day I was told I would be going to Quewest for my safety. I look at father's desk, the one he always sits behind when giving me a lecture. He even sat behind it during our video call when summoning me to come back home and I imagine that he sat there when writing me my weekly emails. That's if he wrote them.
It looks so much smaller now. Funny enough, when I was younger and I did something I wasn't supposed to do like use my strength at a school wrestling match, it's this very desk I feared because I knew that whenever I did something bad, I would be made to sit in front of it and lecture.
I walk over to his liquor cabinet and get a bottle of whiskey.
" You were always curious one when you were young. I see that hasn't changed." A voice behind me says. A voice I remember a lot because he also taught me during some of my gift lessons, Conrad, my father's royal adviser.
He hasn't aged one bit since the last time I saw him.
" Welcome home your highness." He says, bowing before me.

" Please stand up, Conrad. You don't have to bow before me." I tell him, helping him stand.
" But he has too Edward,you're the crown prince of Ambrosia and my only son at that." Father r says entering the study.
I sigh but say nothing,I walk away from the liquor cabinet and sit in the chair I was staring at earlier.
Donovan closes the door behind father and goes straight to the liquor cabinet. He gets two glasses and the bottle of whiskey I had been eying earlier, pours father ran di two drinks before quietly leaving.
" How does it feel to be back home?" Father asks me, handing me a glass of whiskey. I accept it but don't drink any of it.
" It feels weird but fine." I answer him.
" That's to be expected, you haven't been in Ambrosia in over fifteen years." He sits in his favourite chair, taking a sip of the whiskey. Conrad is seated in the corner of the room as always, quiet and observing.
" I see you still won't talk." Father says, probably noticing my thoughts wondered.
" I am talking aren't I, just because I want say a lot doesn't mean I am mute." I answer him.
He always had a problem with me not talking,before mom's death, I was the most talkative and outgoing child and teen but after her death, the will to talk kind of left me.
One of the main reasons father was so accepting of Marshall was because he was the first person I talked to in a really long time.
" Well then I hope you will have more to say during your courtship of Madison." He says, looking at me.
" Do I need to court her, aren't we already engaged?" I ask because I can't for the life of me imagine why she would expect me to court her. She's engaged to me and is to become a princess in the most rich and powerful kingdom of all the four kingdoms. She is already a princess but her father's kingdom is worth ten percent of Ambrosia, that's how rich Ambrosia is.
" You are engaged yes but she expects you to court her, she is a young lady after all. They expect romance and gifts and

what not." He tells me like he is all of a sudden the expert on romances.

I sigh, when I agreed to come back. I thought it was a done deal, start learning from father on how to run the kingdom, marry Madison and shit I don't know I just didn't expect to have to date her or 'court' her as father keeps saying.

" You realise that you have to be married in order to ascend the throne right." Father says breaking my thoughts. It takes a moment for my mind to know what he just said and I almost choke on air.

" Why would I need to ascend?" I ask him carefully. If he means to abdicate, I for one won't stop him. I am just shocked he is thinking of it.

" Edward, you didn't think I would rule forever did you?" I mean I kind of didn't but then again he has been ruling since he was a hundred and forty and he is now two hundred and sixty.

He has built Ambrosia from ground up,when the land was all forests and mines,he built the skyscrapers, hospitals, when the first car was built. I just always assumed he would wait for me to be a hundred at least.

"No I didn't, the news is a bit of a suprise is all." I say. Would I be happy with ascending the throne and becoming king? Yes. A hundred times yes, I have visions for Ambrosia, big ones that I would like to see through.

" You are ready Edward, you will make a great king," father says. I say nothing keeping all my emotions in check.

" Princess Madison and her father will be coming to visit in the next two months. Edward court her and get to know her. You are dismissed."

I stand up and leave. Donovan isn't outside father's office when I leave, he has instead been replaced by a guard I don't. He bows his head in greeting as I pass him.

The crown still sits on my head,a heavy weight and reminder about what lays ahead. Four guards have fallen in step behind me as I walk towards the training ground of the royal guard.

The royal training guard is like an academy, hidden from the rest

of the castle but just as heavily guarded.
I admit to myself that my reasoning for coming here is partly because I want to see Adair in action because she looks as harmless as a fly.
I dismiss the guards following me when I enter because really what harm can happen to me here.
I have never been a fan of the security detail employed by father because they can't harm me but he wants to keep up with appearances so I just roll with it I guess.
I go upstairs in the halls so I can see the training session from above.
The halls are quiet and dark and peaceful, just how I like them.
I stand in a little cove, hidden from view of anyone who can see me but I can see everything happening down the training ground.
" Is he been respectful Leilani, he might be the prince but..." a voice says and I am intrigued. Hearing a private conversation about me isn't something I should be doing but I do it because I know who the voice was addressing.
" But what Donavan? I am okay, don't worry, the prince has been nothing but respectful." Adair tells Donavan, I should have recognized his voice.
" I know the whole ruse of you being his mistress is for his safety but I don't like it, I didn't like it the first time it was suggested and I don't like it. You are my girlfriend and he has a reputation."
I smile at his words and his words confirm my suspicions, he is dating Adair. A little old for her but who am I to judge?
Ok maybe not a little too old but alot to old.
" Donavan I am okay, I don't need you taking care of me, I can take care of myself." She tells him. I am now a little too curious so I take a few steps closer so I can see them.
" I know you can take care of yourself baby but still." I throw up a little at him calling her baby but once again who am I to judge. He has her pinned against the wall, the perv. Adair smiles at him and he leans down as if to kiss her when I think I have had enough of the show so I decide to step out of the little hiding

spot. I watch Adair stiffen in his hands and turn her head when his head leans down and I feel a wave of satisfaction, why I don't know. She quickly steps away from Donavan and bows in greeting,

" Good afternoon Your highness. Are you ready to leave." She asks me. Donavan looks at me with an irritated look on his face and his thoughts are hidden but I don't need to read thoughts to know that cock blocked.

I don't answer Adair's question, I just continue looking at Donavan. I have never been one to rub my power in people's faces but something about Donavan has been rubbing me the wrong way since I arrived.

" Am sorry Donavan but while I was gone did some rules change?" I ask him to completely ignoring air who looks at me with a look of contemplation on her face.

" No your highness or at least none that I am aware of." He replies looking confused.

" Then why didn't you bow when you saw me or are you now above that?" Like I said I am not one to stand on being formal but then again.

If eyes could kill I would be dead but lucky for me they can't and I am immortal so the look Donavan gives me as he kneels down to one eye can't do shit to me.

" I am sorry your highness, you caught me off guard." I ignore him and look at Adair instead,

" I am done for the day, let's go." I turn to leave when a body hits me full speed, hugging me. I am a little aback,

" Edward!!!!" I look down at the person hugging me and smile.

" Mabel, remember who you are talking to." Her brother admonishes.

She stops hugging me, blushing, she takes a step back and bows

" Am sorry your highness, I was very excited to see you." Her jaw clenched and I wanted to laugh. I pull her into my arms and hug her because I missed the shit out of her.

" Mabel, look at you." She smiles and preens at me.

Mabel has grown since I last saw her, gone is the girl I sneaked

kisses with, in front is a woman. A very gorgeous woman.
" Loot at me Edward, look at you." She says eying me with a hungry look in her eyes. One I have become used to over the past years. I hear her thoughts, the ones happy that I am okay, the ones excited that I am back and maybe we can continue where we left off and the one upset with Adair for some reason.
" Your highness, were we not about to leave?" Adair asks me looking irritated and Donavan still looks like he wants me dead.
" Right, Mabel, it was nice to see you but I am afraid I have to leave." I say and I mean it. My life these past few years has been a whirlwind and I am happy to see a familiar face who hasn't changed.
" Okay but you owe me a date Edward, hope you won't run like last time." Mabel says smiling. She bows one last time before walking away Donavan right one her heels.
Well today has indeed been an interesting day.

The Gifted Bloodlines Series Book One

A Court Of Dead Roses

Chapter 5

Edward Vaughn

The last few days have been tiring to say the least. I have been attending court with father, travelling through the city and looking at our family businesses.
I haven't seen much of Marshall as well though he isn't complaining, I leave every morning before he even wakes up.
My gifts have been becoming a lot to handle.
The voices of other people's thoughts are a lot. I could tell father but I know he won't understand so I don't.
I can't explain but it's like my powers are growing which is unheard of.
My only saving grace is that today is the last day of court. No more meetings just working on my own schedule.
I haven't slept much since coming back to Ambrosia. I thought that maybe not living in the castle would help but it hasn't.
The nightmares come more often now and I wake up most days screaming and sweaty.
I am sure Adair hears me but doesn't say anything to save my dignity I guess. Most people would be embarrassed by there guards witnessing them at there lowest but me, I am just glad she me let's be.
I haven't slept at all today, I spent the night looking at the stars through my open window.
My alarm goes off and turn off, wear my work out clothes and head to the gym for my early morning work out.

As always since my arrival back home, I find Adair working out. We have fallen in some kind of routine, her and I.
I find her working in out, don't say a word and join her like to strangers. She doesn't know this but I always watch her. I don't know how many times I have stabbed my toe just watching her run on a treadmill in her little shorts.
I join her like I always do and start running on the treadmill behind her. From the times we have worked out together, I know that running is her favourite form of exercise because it's all she ever does. I have seen her lung weights here and there but for most part she just runs. I love been around though. I think that's partly because her thoughts are a soft voice my head or maybe it's the fact that I feel at peace every time I am with her which isn't a lot of times. The few times we are together is when working out and in the car when going to and from the castle. She also never carries any weapons with her.
Like the first day I worked out with her, I wait until she finishes working out before leaving and as always am winded because fuck.

Since today is the last day of court, Bella is hosting a ball for all members of the court and their families. I didn't want to attend but father insisted that I should. Which has led to this moment right now, me wishing someone would stab me because fuck Marshall talks alot.
" Are sure you don't want the pink one, it brings out your eyes and compliments your blond hair." Marshall asks me, holding a pink tuxedo. The thing is so bloody pink I wonder why the shopper and designer bought it because I couldn't be caught dead in that hideous thing.
" Ok what about this one?" He is now holding an orange and I almost throw up in my mouth. Who the fuck bought these

clothes and the fuck wears an orange tuxedo.
" Why don't you go and get ready? I will take care of my outfit." I tell him as soon as he picks a purple one from the clothing rack.
" And leave you to pick, fuck no. Besides, I already picked out an outfit as soon as they were brought in." Of course he did and am sure he did it earlier than me just to fuck with me.
My personal living room is filled with clothing racks and shoes, courtesy of Bella. She had the clothes so me, Marshall and Adair were dressed to suit the theme.
" Okay, what about this one?" He asks me, this time holding up a yellow one. Oh for fucks sake.
" Actually, Marshall, what about this one?" Adair asks, holding up a dark blue tuxedo that actually looks decent. I didn't hear her come in too busy arguing with Marshall and his terrible fashion sense.
" Yes, that one." I say quickly before Marshall can open his mouth again.
" Oh come on, the ones I picked looked way better." He says looking offended though his thoughts say his fucking with me.
" Yes but this one matches my outfit. The queen invited some of the Ambrosia media." She tells before selecting a dress from the clothing rack and going to her room. Marshall smiles at me with a you are totally fucked look on his face.

I stare at myself in the mirror as I put on my crown. I look alot like mom as I get older. The blond hair, the nose and mouth. The only thing I get from father are my eyes, the color of ember. I wait for my heart to react in any way after thinking about mom but I feel nothing. Sighing in frustration, I walk away from the mirror and leave my room. I head downstairs and find Marshall already dressed and waiting for me in the foyer.
" About time also can I just say how I will never get used to seeing

you with the crown on your head." He says upon seeing me. Well that makes the two of us,I also don't think I will ever get used to feeling its weight in my head.

" But it looks good on you." He continues talking nott waiting for me to answer him, probably because I wasn't going to say anything.

" Do I have to bow before you in public or something because..." he stops talking looking at someone behind me.

When I turn around to look at who has my friend speechless which never happens because Marshall talks a lot and I am instantly speechless even more so than usual.

Adair is a breathtaking sight as she comes down the stairs to the foyer and I am not the only one staring.

Her hair is in loose waves that falls behind her back. She is wearing a silver dress with long sleeves that glimmers when she moves. Her dress has an opening that starts from mid thigh. I don't know much about women's fashion but she looks so goddamn beautiful that I swear my eyes hurt looking.

The other male guards in the room look at her for longer than necessary. Their eyes don't show what they feel but I hear them and I have the strange urge to remove their eyes and feed them to crows.

She walks towards me and I just stand there like an idiot.

" Good evening, your highness." She says bowing. I don't answer her right away, too busy staring like an idiot until Marshall pinches my arm.

" Good evening Adair ahhh," I say stammering, " please stand up, don't bow before me at least for tonight." I tell her with a nervous, clear throat.

" Leilani, you look breathtaking tonight." Marshall tells her, giving her a light kiss on the cheek. Fucking Marshall.

" Don't you agree, Eddy boy?" He asks me with a smirk. Leilani smiles, her eyes lighting up.

" You look lovely Adair." I tell her because she really looks amazing.

" Are you ready, we need to leave because there are so many

people I have to meet at the ball." I ask them both.
" Yes, sorry it took so long to get ready."
" It was worth every moment of being late because you look amazing." I tell her without thinking, ah fuck. Marshall smirks at me, his eyebrows lifting. Leilani smiles but says nothing and I turn around quickly becaus why the fuck did I just say that.
The car to the castle is silent, not that I am complaining because I need all the silence I can get to survive the night.
Marshall is riding in a car alone leaving and Adair alone. She sits quietly playing a game on her phone and all I do is stare at her. She looks good enough to eat in that damn dress of hers and I am thinking about getting a fruit basket to say thank you.
I know that the whole mistress thing is a farce and I respect her but damn does remaining indifferent to her difficult.
It doesn't help that I am going to get engaged in two months and that she has a boyfriend.
" You know staring is rude right?" A voice in my head says and I am startled. I look around the limousine confused, Adair doesn't even look up from her phone.
" I know you can hear or read my thoughts and you don't like talking plus you keep staring at me so I figured why not think about what I want to say that way I don't speak." The voice says again and it takes a second to realise it's Adair's voice I keep hearing.
I try to think of something to say but come up empty so I don't say anything for the rest of the car ride and this time I stop looking at her.
As always when we arrive, she gets off at the guards entrance and I am left alone. I spend what is left of the car ride bracing and building a wall between me and other people's emotions and thoughts.
The car stops and someone opens the door for me. I take a deep breath before getting out. There's so many cameras and flashlights that it takes a few seconds for my eyes to adjust. When I finally open them, I see Ambrosia media waiting to take pictures and make a narrative out of something that isn't there.
I look around for Marshall but I don't see him around so I go

straight inside the inside not stopping to take pictures.

The ballroom is packed to the brim with people, not that I expected anything less.

To be invited to a royal ball is a big deal but to be invited to a royal ball hosted withington the castle grounds is an opportunity to die for or so I have been told.

The orchestra is playing softly in the background while the rich and influential mingle and the social climbers kiss ass.

I see father and Bella and go to greet them.

" Good evening father, you look as lovely as ever Bella." I greet them both. Father nods back in greeting and Bella curtsies with a mega smile on her face. To any onlooker, she looks posed and is the epitome of grace but I know better. Her nerves are all over place because this is her first time meeting me but I don't pay her any attention.

I stand beside and wait as every invited guest comes and pays their respects before going to enjoy the party.

My eyes scan the crowd and I see a few familiar faces. Leilani is on Donavan's hand, smiling politely at something he says is saying the perfect couple to any onlooker. Mabel is a guard. I don't recognize all dressed up in order to blend in and be part of the guests. To everyone here, the only security detail are the ones standing in all the corners of the room, watching the guests but the royal guards are part of the guests, watching for any signs of trouble and ready to jump in at any given moment. I see Marshall flirting with one of the guests, a redhead from lord knows where not that Marshal will care.

" Why don't you ask lord Percival's daughter to dance, Edward." Father tells me. I want to ask but that's too big a word for him. I nod before seeking the girl out. She giggles when I ask her and accepts right before she spends the next ten minutes stepping on my toes.

She talks alot about the most nonsensical consequential things that I am so glad when I can finally dump her back with her father.

I look around the room for Marshall but I don't see him or the

redhead. Which only means he managed to sneak out, the lucky fucker.
" You owe me a date, your highness." A voice besides me says,
I turn to look at Mabel,who looks as lovely as ever.
" Now how could I forget that?" I ask her, flirting a little.
" I don't know, you tell me." She answers me with a smile in her voice. I see father walking towards me with another lord or some shit.
" Dance with me." I say pulling Mabel to the dance floor.
" Still running from daddy dearest I see." She tells me, looking over my shoulder at my father who has now stopped and is talking to some ass kisser.
The thing with my family is we are so rich that there is literally nothing you can bribe us with. We own almost all the important things in Ambrosia so most ass kissers want part of the wealth or to be simply associated with the royal family. Me and Marshall had a hard time starting our private company from ground up especially since no one knows I own part if it bit we did. Though sometimes I am still in shock about the whole thing.
" Not running, merely dancing with a beautiful woman who keeps on complaining about the date I swindled her out of." I say smoothly with a smile. Mabel laughs at this,
" Still a flirt I see. At least the media got that part right." She says, I sigh dramatically,
" Reading and listening to gossip about me, are we Mabel Hope." I ask her teasing.
" Yes Edward, out of curiosity and to see how you were. You left without a word and I was worried sick about you." She tells me her voice changes from light and teasing to serious.
I don't want to talk about my leaving so I just stop talking instead. We dance around the dance floor for a few more minutes before Mabel leaves me to mingle and work because unlike me today, she's working and protecting Bella.
My shield is scrambling and I can feel it, a few voices breaking the wall I formed around myself so I quickly go outside in the garden.

There are a few people outside, a few guards here and there but it's mostly empty and I find myself breathing a little easier.

I feel Adair before I see her, I don't know how or why but I have developed an awareness whenever I am around her.

" You know leaving the ball room full of people without telling me makes my job harder than necessary right?" She asks, coming to stand beside me. She's nursing a glass of champagne, the same one she's been holding for the last two hours I think maybe since getting here.

" Sorry, to many people in there, I just needed a minute to myself." I say.

She looks lovely under the moonlight. Like a dream, too good to be true. We continue standing in silence, looking at the moonlight. Adair is swaying softly to the music being played inside the ball room. I hear some voices approaching us, talking about me. I might be getting engaged in a few months but to every single lady here I am fair game hence the reason I left the ballroom. Their thoughts are all the same, who can get me to fall in 'love' with them and what not.

" Do you want to dance?" I ask Adair, she blinks in surprise and makes a face probably about to say no when I pull her in my arms not waiting for a response. What the fuck is wrong with me and pulling ladies to dance with me.

" I am holding a glass of champagne, making it kind of hard to dance with you, your highness." She says looking for a way out of dancing with me. I grab her glass and throw it behind me,it lands with a soft thud and doesn't break because of the soft grass it landed on.

" There. Problem fixed now, dance with me, please." I say, pulling her close. I put my hands around her waist and she shivers a little when my fingers touch the bare skin of her back.

" You know running away from them and avoiding them just makes you more desirable, more mysterious." She says with a smirk on her face, clearly finding my discomfort entertaining. I grant in response. Adair puts her hands on my shoulders and we start moving slowly to the song the orchestra is playing.

The voices I heard earlier stumble upon us but leave immediately after when a guard ushers them back with some excuse and we are alone once again only now Adair is in my arms.

" Thank you." I say softly over the top of her head acknowledging the fact that the guard did that because she asked him too, how I don't know but I am grateful.

" No problem, you need a breather." She says simply.

This is the closest I have ever been to her excluding the kiss in front of the media that is.

My hands drift up her back feeling and touching more of her skin which is soft to touch. She shivers again but doesn't pull back so I keep on exploring, tracing her asking and making drawing patterns as we dance. She finally stops looking over my shoulder as we dance and looks up at me, her hazel eyes shining under the moonlight.

I continue my exploration and pull flush against me. Her breasts are pressed up against my chest and I internally curse myself for wearing a three piece suit because I could give my left hand to feel her pressed against me. Her hands drift up my shoulders until I feel her fingers on the nape of my neck, her fingers playing with my hair.

Caught in a moment of weakness my wall crumbles and my grip on her tightens. Fuck. The voices come, a lot of them at once, like screaming banshees all in my head. Adair winces probably because I am hurting her but doesn't say anything. She gasps softly before pulling my head down and kissing me.

The kiss is unexpected but a welcome distraction from everything going on.

Her lips are soft against mine. For the first few seconds I stand frozen as she kisses me but when I sense her start to pull back, I take over and deepen the kiss. Unlike the kiss last time, I am in full control and I slip my tongue in her mouth, nipping softly at her lower lip. She sighs in my mouth and I know I am doing something right. She tastes of chocolate, her mouth sweet with a little bitterness that dark chocolate poses. My left hand leaves her back and drifts lower to her ass which I grab and use to hold her tightly against me. Her grip on my knack tightens and we kiss like people starved. She bites my lower lip, taking just as I am giving and I drown in the kiss.

Adair pulls back suddenly, I try to kiss her but she steps back.

" Am sorry your highness but that was the only way to distract, your eyes turned and well they are still red, like a flame." My walls crumbling must have caused that. I close my eyes and blink, opening them again I look at Adair silently asking her if they have changed back,

" No still the same, listen follow me I can't risk anyone seeing you like this." I nod and follow her.

She leads me away from the ballroom and on to a path that leads us to the woods and everything is a blur.

The voices in my head are back in full force, her kissing me helped distract me but only for a little while and I can feel my nails changing. It's like I am a balloon filled with so much aid that I might explode at any given minute.

Somehow we end up in a car garage, my head is hurting like a raging beast and my nose is starting to bleed so I don't even question Adair when she gets into a car that wasn't the one we arrived in. I climb into the car and sit in the passenger's seat.

" This is going to be a bumpy ride so get ready." Adair tells me, looking at me through the rearview mirror, I nod as I try to get my breathing under control.

The castle grounds are huge but somehow Adair manages to drive out without me being seen like she's done it a thousand times and I don't question her, as long as we leave the castle grounds and go where there's a few or no people at all.

I try to get my breathing under control and try to rebuild the walls in my mind but fail. I feel like I am on fire and my nails are all but claws now.

I am not sure how long we are in the car nor am I aware of my surroundings until my door is opened.

I breathe a lot better when the cool night air hits my face. I hear the faint calming sound of water and immediately open my eyes

because that's all I hear.
Adair is looking at me with a concerned expression on her but I don't say a word, I simply get out of the car.
She drove us to a forest, the car is parked a few meters away from a little waterfall. You can see the moon properly from here without the city lights obscuring it or the lights from the castle but most importantly, its empty and my mind is my own again.
I start stripping off my clothes so I can get into the water to calm down.
" What are you doing?" Adair asks me. Fuck I forgot about her.
" What does it look like I am doing, stripping so I can go for a swim? I feel like my body is on fire." I tell her, unbuckling my belt.
" Oh okay, I will just sit over there and wait for you then." She says pointing at the grass on the banks of the stream or whatever this place is.
I don't answer her, I just finish unbuttoning my shirt, take off my socks and shoes leaving me only in boxer briefs before I jump in the stream.
The water is so fucking cold that if I didn't feel so bloody hot I am sure my balls would have shrivelled up and fell off.
I start feeling the change in me, I don't build my walls up again but only because I don't have to. My mind is an open play field for anyone's voice to wander in but I don't hear or feel anyone for miles away, not even Adair.
My claws go back in and I am instantly grateful my teeth didn't make an unwanted appearance.
I swim for a few minutes before I am back to normal and then I start swimming towards the shore. I find Adair where I left her only now she's not wearing any shoes.
" I am sorry if I made you uncomfortable, my gifts have been out of control of late." I say, walking out of the water once I have reached the shallow ends.
" You didn't make me uncomfortable, your highness, although next time you decide to strip in front of me, do it with some finesse, it's not every day I get to see you naked." She says with a

smile in her voice.

I laugh at her little joke, happy I didn't scare her away.

" Don't worry, next time I decide to strip in front of you, I will do a little dance." I answer her, coming to sit next to her.

" That you should be your highness, that you should." She says looking up at the moon.

" Please Adair, after the night we have had don't you think you can finally drop the your highness and call me by my given name." Becaus fuck it all, after that kiss, I don't want her calling me by my royal title at all.

" Okay," she says looking at me,

" Vaughn it is though it might take a lot of getting used to."

No one ever calls me Vaughn, only my mother did. I want to ask her not to me Vaughn but to call me Edward but I don't because somehow it just feels right.

" Your eyes are still glowing red, Vaughn." She breaks my thoughts.

" Oh sorry about that," I say blinking.

" They are always the last to turn back to normal." I remember the first time they turned, I spent the whole morning in my room looking at them because I thought they were the most beautiful eyes then father came and made me change them back because well, I would scare the mortals and reveal our secret.

" Don't worry about it, they are beautiful." She tells me looking back up at the moon.

" Thank you." Mom also thought they looked nice but well father had more of a point.

" How does it feel?" She asks me suddenly,

" How does what feel?" I say confused.

" To be able to read people's thoughts, to transform or use any of your gifts, how does it feel?" She looks at me curiously and all I feel is curiosity from her.

" Well the mind reading isn't exactly mind reading, it's more like mind hearing. I don't read your thoughts, it's like I hear your voice in my head only you don't open your mouth and it tells me your thoughts. Some are calm and collected but most of them

are like a thousand banshees screaming in my ears." I say.
I don't know what has been wrong with me since arriving. It's like being back in Ambrosia has multiplied the power of my gifts or something because my walls have never cracked to let in that many thoughts. Some of my ancestors died because of that, we might be immoral but any damage to the brain is the death of us.
" That sounds painful." She says with a wince.
" It is, thank you for your quick thinking with the kiss." I look at her expecting her to blush but she doesn't.
" You are welcome, the pleasure was all mine anyway, you are a good kisser."
She stands up and walks towards the car. Her comment on me being a good kisser stings, I mean I know I am good but all the women I have been with or kissed always say I am the best. I know it's true because even there thoughts told me but to her I am merely good.
" Come on Vaughn, before Donavan sends out a search party for you."
I gather my clothes and get in the back seat of her car. *You are a good kisser* my ass. I will kiss Adair again and this time around I will be better than good.

Chapter 6

Edward Vaughn

The car ride is quiet, not the awkward silence,no just peaceful silence.

When we get back to my house, there's no search party. Adair had suggested if everything is normal, nothing out of the ordinary.

Guards come and open the door for me as soon as Adair parks the car. Someone gets the cars from her to properly park the car.

" Good night Vaughn, it was nice dancing with you." Adair says as she goes inside, leaving me behind. I smirk,

" The pleasure was all mine." She laughs and touches my shoulder, her hand cool against my still warm skin,

" Get some sleep, you have had a long night." I watch her walk up the stairs like a love struck fool.

I wait for the ringing headache I had before to come back now that I am near people again but nothing happens. No ringing, no voices, just blessed silence.

" May I take your clothes, your highness?" A maid asks me.

I nod, handing her my jacket, shirt, shoes and stockings, leaving me in my trousers.

∞∞∞

I lay awake staring up at my ceiling. I have been in bed trying to sleep for last four hours since I came home close to midnight the night before. But nothing, I want to say it's insomnia but I know I would be lying to myself.

Whenever I close my eyes I am back running, being hunted down like a bloody animal. Most of my dreams, I fail to run, I keep on falling and falling and it seems all too real so I have opted for not sleeping at all.

Sighing I get out of bed and grab my canvas. Before mom's death, drawing and painting always calmed me down. Sure I wasn't as good as her but I wasn't terrible either.

I set it up near my window so I can have a perfect view of the moon and stars.

I grab my paint brush, dip in paint and force myself to paint something.

I stroke the brush up and down the blank canvas a few times before getting frustrated and breaking the damn thing in half.

Any other artist or painter would have been inspired by the view before me but not me. It's like all my art died with mom on that damned day.

Fuck!!!!!!

I break my canvas in half and smash it against the wall. Fuck!!!

I start punching the wall, my knuckles bloody but I don't care. Fuck.

I don't realise I am screaming and crying until a soft body comes and hugs me, pulling me close.

She smells of roses, red roses. She sits down pulling me down with her. She holds my body as I cry and sob, saying nothing. Sobs rack my body and I let it out. I want to say I know why I am crying but I don't but I don't question myself either because it feels like an enormous pressure has been lifted off me so I cry.

Adair holds me until I can't cry anymore because I have nothing left to give. She helps me to my bed, covers me without saying a word. She closes the blinds on my windows, takes my alarm and leaves me to sleep. I sleep too exhausted to fight.

∞∞∞

When I wake the sun is shining brightly like a silent fuck you to my face. I check the time on my phone and see that it's 1pm in the afternoon. Fuck, that's the longest I have slept I a while.

My room is still a mess,the broken canvas still a mess on the floor, blood splattered against the walls, some of it a dry mess on my knuckles.

My knuckles have healed already, the pain only temporarily.

I take off my clothes and get into the shower. The hot sprays of water are a welcome distraction from everything else that's going on right now.

I haven't cried in a while, fifteen years to be exact or felt the way I did last night. My heart turned numb when mom died. It's like I am a teenager all over again going through emotions I don't understand and that scares me.

Growing up father has always taught me that a king doesn't cry, that emotion is beneath us because why love when whoever you love will eventually die and leave you alone with your immortality.

After mom died I took his advice. The only people I have let get close to me are Marshall and his mother, I wouldn't say I love them but I am fond of them.

I wash the dried blood off my knuckles, remembering last night. One second I was trying to paint, then the next I was punching hole through the wall.

I would have stayed like that if it wasn't for her.

I didn't hear her open my door, I just felt her. I didn't see her through my own tears but she sat with me as I cried and didn't say a word, she just sat and rocked me. She smelled of roses last night, a fresh blooming rose.

A scent I hate and associate with mom since she always smelled of it is roses. It has always reminded me of the roses I watched

die because I hadn't learnt to heal yet.
Until last night the scent of roses made me want to throw up because if I had stayed indoors that afternoon and learnt to heal, mastered my gift maybe mom would still be here, maybe just maybe life would.bw different.
But last night, it was a welcome distraction, I didn't want to throw up, I wanted to be part of it, to be part of her, her warmth. I wanted to inhale the whole bloody bottle of her perfume just so I can smell the roses some more.
I stand under the shower until my skin starts to prune and looks pink before turning off the water.
I get a towel and dry myself before going to my wardrobe and getting something to wear.
After all the meetings at court the first week of been back, I finally have a few days to myself and I need them because fuck it I don't think I ama good company at the moment.
It's a relatively warm day so I wear some grey sweatpants and slides, grab my phone and a book then go outside.
One of the reasons I built my house here is because of its location, in the middle of forest and nature.
A few servants bow as I walk by and I see guards stationed everywhere but I don't see any signs of Marshall or Adair.
" Good afternoon, your highness." A guard greets me, Reginald. I think I heard Adair call him.
" Good afternoon, where's Marshall?" I ask him.
" Oh, by the pool with Leilani. I was told to tell that once you awakened." I nod to him before going to the pool.
I value my privacy above all else so the pool is a good ten minutes walk away from the house, hidden and secure so no unwanted security detail is needed. All I want to do is relax, read my book and eat something because I am starving.
I hear Marshall and Adir talking before I see them.
Adair is seated underneath an umbrella chair, wearing a blue bikini which makes me internally vow to myself that I won't look at her while Marshall does laps around the pool.
" Look who has finally decided to grace us with his presence." He

says sarcastically as soon as he sees me.
" Good afternoon to you too, Marshall." I say sitting next to Adair. Adair hands me a bowl of fruit and a glass of juice without even looking at me,
" Thank you. I need the food after the night I have had." I say putting my book down. Marshall continues swimming and it's like the conversation they had been having earlier is over. It isn't supposed to hurt me but it does because I want Adair to talk to.me they way she talks to Marshall or that Reginald guard, but it's like whenever she's around all she says are a few words when she's spoken too making me want to talk more than i usually want to.
" Thank you, for last night." I find myself telling her, it's like when I am around her my brain forgets how to bloody work because I find it doing more actions without consulting me first.
" Which part, the first or second time?" She asks me, finally looking at me.
" Both times." I say simply because she did help me alot last night.
" You're welcome." She says smiling at me.
I look at her thoughtfully as I eat my fruits. Royal guards get paid and make a lot of money but she had me vulnerable both times, so why didn't she take advantage. She could have taken pictures of me both times or videos and sold them to the highest bidder because a lot of people in the four kingdoms would pay to see my father and I destroyed but she didn't.
" Why did you help me when you could have made thousands with a video of me breaking down like that?" I ask, she could have been rich and run away. I would have done it had our positions been reversed.
" I could have made millions Vaugh, not thousands but I didn't because well, it would have been taking advantage of you when you are most vulnerable." She tells me, standing up,
" I like fair fights." She says, getting a strawberry from my bowl of fruit.
I watch her chew the strawberry, some of the strawberry juice

dripping down her chin and I feel myself get hard, fuck. She smirks at me,
" You have a visitor." She says before walking away. I watch her as she jumps into the pool, transfixed.
" Good afternoon Edward." Mabel greets me. I look at her surprised only to realize that Adair had told me that I had a visitor before she went for her swim.
" Good afternoon Mabel. How has your morning been?" I ask hd as she takes the seat Adair had just vacated.
" It's been okay, today is my day off and I knew you weren't going to man up and take me on my date so I decided to pass by."She says.
She's probably right. Mabel was a big part of my life before the death of my mom, a constant figure really. I don't know how many times we snuck out, going on our little dates or our late night snacks when she would sneak food for me knowing I probably hadn't had any food. Like I said, a huge part of my life.
I feel bad for ignoring her though it hasn't been intentional but still, I left hd without any explanation, the least I can do is go on a date with her as she has been telling me since she saw me. We can catch up so I can know how life has been for her.
" Okay. Where do you want us to go, I haven't been in Ambrosia in a long time." I ask her, eating my fruits.
" Well I can't exactly take you anywhere outside of your house because of the security detail but I honestly just want to spend the day with you I guess." Securing has always been tight hence sneaking around when we were teens.
" I will be with you, doesn't that count as security?" I ask, again not that I need it but then again,
" I am but I can't, I report to Leilani and Donavan. I can't just leave with you." I choke on an orange,
" You report to Adair?" I ask, genuinely shocked but mostly out of curiosity. Mabel laughs nervously,
" Yes I do, I thought you knew." She's not looking at me when talking but staring at Adair instead who is still doing laps around the pool.

" I didn't, I don't like the security father and the royal counsel employ already so it's just there, I don't ask about it and that's it." I tell her honestly.

We are both staring at Adair now but I am sure for very different reasons.

" She's a tough one. When she first tried out, I was with her. I grew up in the castle grounds, obviously training and goofing around. When I tried to try out after I turned eighteen, Donovan told me not to. Asked me to go to school and what not, I wanted to argue obviously but I didn't. I went to school, then came back to try out for the royal guard when I was thirty and she was sixteen." She's still not looking at but rather at the water in the pool as she talks,

" We all thought what the fuck is a sixteen year old going to do here, that it was going to be a walk over," she laughs a little as she says this, " We where so wrong. The kid almost killed Reginald in bare knuckle boxing during the first week of training. Reginald was embarrassed but weirdly enough, he took her piek a young sister I guess. They are always together," she smiles this time, " I won't list I hate her, give me the chance and I would probably kill her but I respect her and she's seen Donavan so I have to be nice though she doesn't need protecting." She says with a chuckle.

Adair, now tired of swimming, gets out of the pool. I watch her again, she looks like a goddess coming out of a bath. Her hair, which is normally a mess of curls and waves is now tamed and wet, her bikini leaving very little to my imagination and I watch mesmerized. I envy the little droplets of water that cling to her skin, wishing it was ms instead. I watch as she grabs a towel, drying herself and I feel myself getting hard. I stifle a groan because fuck it all she's killing me which is ironic considering she's doing nothing but drying herself. At this rate, I swear I could watch Adair do nothing but breath and still be turned on.

" Staring is rude." A voice admonishes in my mind. I swallow looking up to find Adair staring at me, she smirks before turning and walking in the other direction of the pool. She seats in on the beach chairs there, a place where I can see her but where she has

also given me privacy to swat and talk to Mabel.
I want to think about how she can get in my head especially considering the fact that I haven't heard any other thoughts since waking up this morning but I don't, I just stare at her trying to figure out the puzzle which is Leilani Adair.
" Stare any more lover boy and the poor girl might just hit her head or something." Mabel says, looking at me. I cough nervously but say nothing to defend myself.
" She's that good of a guard then. That explains her being asked to personally guard me then." I say changing the topic from my staring and back to Adair.
" She's the best. She was born with a killer's instinct and is good at what she does, she became a royal guard on first try and became a keeper six months later beating Donavan's record. That's how good she is." Mabel says with a little envy in her voice. " Also making her the first woman keeper since a long time ago. When we thought that you would be coming back and the potential of you being attacked, I came up with the idea of you having a fake mistress considering your reputation and she was picked to do it by your father himself."
Wow. It's very hard to become a keeper, especially a woman but she did it. I am oddly proud of her, why? I don't know.
" Anyway enough about Leilani, let's talk about you and your ladies' man reputation." Mabel says changing the topic.
I let him change the topic but my mind is still stuck on Adair and all I have learnt about her today.
I spend the rest of the day with Mabel and Marshall drinking and catching up. By the end of the day, I am glad I had this date with Mabel, she's always been a friend of mine before anything else.

Chapter 7

Edward Vaughn

I am running again. I have always been a good runner, but somehow today I keep on falling and I can't run for more than a few feet before falling.
Someone is chasing me. I don't know who it is, all I know is that I have to run inorder to survive. I hear her scream, her scream deadly. I don't think I will be able to forget only now that it sounds different. I stop running to look at the person who screamed and find myself staring into hazel eyes. The eyes are usually filled with laughter or like we share some kind of secret stare at ms lifeless.
I wake up screaming. Fuck.
My bed feels wet to touch, probably from all the sweating I did.
I had another nightmare again, only today it was different. When I turned to look at mom, it was Adair u saw. The dream shook me. I stand up and walk in steadily on my legs, shivering when I remember the lifeless look her eyes had to them. Fuck, fuck, fuck.
I need something to take my mind off my dream. I look at my watch and see that it's 4am. I decide to go to the gym earlier than usual, better really, than staying up in my room alone with my thoughts.

∞∞∞

Adair is sitting by the window this time around, reading a book. Her hair is in a messy bun, and she's wearing a hoodie that looks large on her, her legs crossed munching on a bar of chocolate. This is the first time I have seen her look like this, with her guard down. She looks at peace. I stand and stare like a creep because when it comes to her,I don't seem to have manners.

" Staring is rude." She says,not bothering to look up from her book.

It doesn't surprise me that she heard me enter the gym though, with her I am always in for a surprise.

" I can't seem to help myself," I grinning like an idiot, " Good morning Adair." I'm going to sit next to her.

" Good morning Vaughn." She puts her book down to look at me, " You're up earlier than usual."

She looks at me curiously, taking a bite out of her bar of chocolate.

" I couldn't sleep." Simply, she sleeps in the room next to mine and considering what happened the other night, I am sure she has heard me scream other times.

" Ah, I now don't know what to say." She gets a bottle of water I didn't notic before and takes a sip.

" I don't expect you to say anything." I say this because I really don't.

" I know. You know for someone who doesn't talk much, you seem to have a lot to say when you're around me."

She's looking at me thoughtfully, like I am some weird creature she just discovered.

It's true I don't like to talk and when I was fifteen right after the death of my mom, I preferred not to do that until I met Marshall. He got me to talk but that's about the extent of it.

Coming back to Ambrosia, I didn't think I would be fine but then I met Adair and that seemed to change things. I don't tell her that the only people I actually talk to or carry conversations with are her, Marshall and Mabel. Though with her it's different, with her I deliberately seek her out to talk, with her I want to talk, I

want to laugh and I want to smile.
" Only when I am around you." Is all I say, she can take it how she likes.
" Okay." She stands up and starts to take off her hoodie and u watch her like the creep I am becoming. She's in her shorts and sports bra again. Is it just me or do those get smaller every fucking day. She puts her hoodie on the floor next to me and heads for the treadmill,her break over I guess. I pick up the book she had been reading, a novel. I don't remember the last time I read one of those.
I flip through the pages until I find the one she had been reading. I didn't know the kind of book she had her little nose stuck in until I read the first line on the page she had been reading.
" Shut up and suck it like a whore."
I choke and start coughing, what the fuck.
" You have a system of being nosy, your highness." She says laughing. She's no longer running but is now laughing and staring at me as I cough trying to clear my wind up of the saliva that decided today would be a great day to take a different route.
Adair has the most amazing laugh. It's melodic and if i was ever into music, I would record and listen to her laugh over and over again because well she sounds like an angel.
" Are these the kind of books you read?" I ask her, after I finally catch my breath.
" I read all sorts of books," she says with a smirk, " those just happen to be my favourite." She starts laughing again. I put the book down because reading while I am alone in a room with Adair is dangerous.
The thought of Adair reading such turns me on so fucking much. She's stopped laughing and is back to running on the treadmill. She's a free spirit, this one,full of surprises that it angers me that a woman like her is with a man like Donavan.
Donavan is a good man but I just don't like or trust him, which is funny because I didn't really care much about him until I met Adair. They haven't been alone again since the day in the corridor. That gives me a little peace because the thought of him

alone with Adair makes me angry. I want to be the only man she smiles or laughs for.
" It's a good book." I tell her after my prolonged silence.
" How would you know, you have only read a few lines and choked." She counters. I mean she's not wrong but I choked due to the shock of what she had been reading, not the book itself.
" I choked because I was shocked by the kind of book you are reading, not the words I read." I tell her trying to salvage what's left of my pride.
" Of course you did." Her words say one thing but the way she said the words tells another story.
" I can read your whole book and not break a sweat Adair, I was just surprised, is all."
" Hey, I believe you. You're the one trying to prove it to me when there is really nothing to prove." She gets off the treadmill and comes to stand in front of me. Her standing and ms sitting puts me on the same level as her belly button but she's standing a few feet away. My imagination gets the better of me and I don't realise that she is talking to me until she taps my shoulder.
" Vaughn did you hear what I just said." Fuck me.
" No,I'm sorry , please repeat that." I ask her. She looks at me funny but does as I ask her.
" I am taking the night off today, the guards here will be in charge of your security." Oh, I wasn't expecting that.
" Ok, going out?" I ask partly because I am curious and partly because I don't want her to go and see Donavan after reading her little book. Which sounds irrational considering Donavan is her boyfriend.
" No, I just need a break." She bends down and starts picking her things, starting with her little book.
" Okay, sure, take the night off, I will be fine." I tell her, not sure who I am trying to assure.
" Okay then, thank you." She leaves and I watch her walk away.

∞∞∞

I am in my living room, watching a movie when the door to Adair's bedroom opens.

She steps out wearing Jean shorts. I think I am not sure what they are called but they show a lot of her bum cheeks, a shirt that only covers her boobs. Her hair is a mass of curls and her lips are painted red. She looks amazing, effortlessly so. She stops when she sees me.

" Good evening Vaughn." I turn down the volume on the tv,

" Good evening Adair."

We look at each other in awkward silence for a few seconds before she breaks it.

" Is this all you're doing tonight?" He seems to be genuinely curious. I want to lie and say no, I have something to do but I don't lie. I am young any more and the only thing important to me at the moment is taking over from father when he abdicates. Not that I ever did anything interesting when I was her age.

" No, I will watch this movie before going to sleep." I say, answering her question.

" Let's go out." She says,

" Pardon?" I ask her, taken aback by her request.

" Let's go out. You will be here cooped up for the evening and I am going out, let's go out. I will be your guide for the night." She looks happy with her suggestion.

I want to day, yes but then I also don't want to impose on her on her free night. Being a keeper is hard work but mine isn't really hard but still she deserves the night out.

" Oh, thank you but I wouldn't want to impose." I tell her being honest.

" Oh you won't be imposing, besides the more the merrier." She comes to stand next to the couch I am sitting on.

" Come on,it will be fun. No one will know where you are and I will be there in case we get into trouble or something, come on Vaughn let's go." I start to get up but hesitate,

" Come on Vaughn, you will be fine. But can you wear something else." She smiles after saying the last part.

What the heck, what's the worst that could happen. I go and change wearing black jeans and black button down shirt.
" I am ready, let's go." I say leaving my room.
Adair is still standing where I left her. She looks at my outfit, inspecting if I meet her approval and nodding.
" Don't you look handsome." She says nodding. I roll my eyes at her,
" You look really nice." She tells me laughing at my eye roll.
" Come on Adair, are we going or not?" I ask her.
" We are only well now, we have a problem." She says, looking at me.
" What?" I ask now irritated but I don't show it though I am sure she knows.
" Well, where are we going? I don't want the whole ' here come his highness' security and your whole parade of security, no offence." She says after I change the expression on my face.
" None taken." I assure you, besides I know what she means. The whole process is frustrating at best so I understand.
" Good so well we have to sneak out, you will be fine because I can handle any surprises we come by. How good are you at jumping?" She asks.
She told me about my safety if at all we do this and I am more worried about how my blue balls will fare especially if I intend to spend the night out with her.
" I understand but does my knowing how to jump have anything to do with this?" I ask her.
" Well I was hoping you would be able to jump out of your window and I can find you outside the car park."
I chuckle at her statement. I haven't sneaked out of my room in a while and everytime I did it, it was for some reason Adair is asking me to do it for now.
" Don't worry about me, I will walk out with you but no one will see me."
Adair opens her mouth, probably about to argue but I don't wait for her to say anything.
Like I always do before using any of my gifts, I reach down deep

and start gathering my strength. I feel it build up in me, I free myself unleashing all my locked up powers. I know it's working when Adair gasps in the background.
" Did it work?" I ask her.
" It did. Fuck I forgot you could do that, wow. Although next time a little heads up will be nice." She looks astonished but sounds upset. I laugh at her though I don't blame her for being upset, after all it's not every day a person becomes invisible in front of you.
" You just disappeared into thin air, like you weren't there to begin with, are you around and if you are, am I facing you right now?" She was still surprised, her mouth still slightly open.
" No, I moved." I answer her and turn towards the sound of my voice,
" Come on, you said something about not being caught so let's go." I say.
" How am I supposed to know where you are when walking?" She makes a fair point.
I go and stand behind her and gently brush her hair behind her ear,
" Just cause you can't see me doesn't mean you can't feel me." I say, whispering in her ears.
She gasps and her cheeks turn pink. I smirk to myself before holding her hand,
" Come on, you're the one who wanted me to come along." I tell her.
She snaps out of her trance and starts pulling me behind her,
" Ok Vaughn, full of party tricks. I hope you can keep up."
We walk out of my suite together and Adair leads the way like a woman on a mission. She stops and closes the door behind her before talking to one of the guards stationed just outside my door,
" The prince is sleeping, he says he's had a long day and doesn't wish to be disturbed. Don't." Her voice is commanding and the guard nods at her orders before resuming his earlier position. I wait until we are out of ear shot of the guards before whispering

in her ears again,
" So commanding Adair, had I known this is how you would be, I would have left with you the first time you asked me." I tease. She snorts but says nothing.
We meet a few guards in the hallway, all of them nodding at Adair in respect and I find myself admiring her. She has accomplished so much at such a young age. We head down the stairs but stop short before we can leave the front door, Adair starts talking to another guard, this one stationed at the front door.
" I am leaving Daniel, bullshit till I get back. Bye."
We walked towards the car park.
" You can let go of my hand now Vaughn, I hope you can get into the car without my help." She tells me. I let go of her hand and follow her.
We pass all my cars until we reach a black Harley that's been parked separately. I whistle, admiring the beauty before me.
" You like to live life on the edge." I observe. Adair smirks at thin air and I laugh at her quickly holding it in when I see one of the guards turn towards the sound of my voice.
" Shit, I am sorry, it's just that you are looking in the wrong direction." I am standing on her left hand side but she was looking in front of her.
" Just climb on behind me before you get us, Vaughn. I will give you a helmet once we are a distance away, don't want people to see a floating helmet now do we." She says climbing on the motorcycle.
I sit behind her and hold her waist. I don't expect my hands to touch soft skin. She shivers at my touch but says nothing. She turns on the engine and I grip her waist.
She rides the bike down my driveway towards the gate and I enjoy the feel of her in my arms. The gates open for us and I release a breath I didn't know I had been holding when we leave.
We ride for twenty minutes before Adair stops and parks the bike.
" Ok, you can change back now." She tells me without turning

around.

I get off the bike and stand in the grass nearby and start turning back.

I can do it at the flick of a wrist but then I haven't been able to use my gifts a lot in the last few years.

" That was fast." Adair comments.

" Turning a gift on is more difficult than turning it off." I say simply. She nods before handing me a mask I didn't even know she had.

" Wear this," I look at the half mask that covers half my face from my hairline to my nose.

" Why do I have to wear it." I ask her,

" Well, i have sneaked out without your security but that doesn't mean people where we are going won't know you."

Makes sense I guess. I wear the mask, tying the strings behind my head.

Adair then hands me a helmet and I put it on without a word.

She turns on the engine of the bike and I get on the back again.

We ride and I hold on to her. I mostly like holding her.

I enjoy looking at the passing scenery whilst breathing in the now familiar scent of roses she always seems to smell of.

We soon reach the city or rather the heart of it.

I haven't been here since coming back and I behave like a tourist, busy staring at everything around me in awe.

" I have managed to sneak you out, you falling off my bike and cracking your head open isn't part of my plans so please hold on to me." Adair tells me in my head, her voice sarcastic. I snort and tighten my hold around her waist.

She soon parks her bike behind a building that looks abandoned. We get off the take and take off our helmets. She puts on a mask of her own before turning to look at me.

" I know how hard it is for you to be around so many people so just a heads up, there's a lot of people here but most of them won't bother you. They are here to let loose so all their thoughts are a little less aggressive."

I smile at her words,flattered she listens and cares enough. I want to tell her that whenever I am with her, she's like a soothing voice cancelling the others but I don't, I simply nod in understanding.

" Don't leave my side please, let's go." She tells me before turning around and walking towards the building I am still suspicious of.

I walk closely behind her. She knocks on the door and a person wearing a mask opens it for her, he nods at her and allows to enter.

The inside is lit, not bright enough where it makes your head hurt but bright enough where you can see around you. There are people dancing, drinking, talking and laughing but none of them pay us any mind. I feel the atmosphere and energy surrounding me and it's like Adair had said, carefree and happy.

Adair takes my hand and pulls me through the throngs of people dancing on the dance floor to the other side of the room.

This one is less crowded. She leads me to a table with only two people sitting there and I recognize the guard named Reginald immediately behind his mask.

Adair leans over to hug him and the woman his was seated with before taking a seat and sit next to her.

" I thought you would never come." The woman says to Adair. She's talking to Adair but her eyes are on me as are Reginald's.

" Sorry I'm late, something came up that I had to take care of." She says, taking a drink from the one that we find on the table,

" This is my friend, no name." She tells her friends referring to me and I snort a laugh at her imagination. Her elbow jabs my ribs and I stop laughing,

" Anyway, he doesn't want to be disturbed so don't bother him."

Reginald looks at me for a long uncomfortable moment before looking away and I know that he recognizes me but picks to ignore me all together.

The woman with him looks at me before turning back to Adair.

" Okay, I am just happy you dropped Donavan like a hot sack of potatoes." I decide that I like right there and then. Adair looks at her with a smirk,

" Who said I dropped him?" I find myself clenching my fist at her statement but say nothing.

" Lei, the man is twice your age and an asshole, now I love him and I trust your judgement but I don't get your attraction to him at all." Her friend says,sipping her drink.

I stop looking at them lest I appear interested in their conversation.

" So you have said since you found out about him Klara," Adair says.

Klara sighs and drops the topic which is a daily occurrence. I find that I like Klara immensely.

Reginald stands up and lifts Klara who laughs after she's lifted and walks away with her.

" I am sorry you had to hear that. Would you like a drink?" Adair asks me.

" No, I am ok, what is this place?" I ask, my gaze curiously looking around the bar.

" Well I am sure you have gathered that it's a bar." She answers,

" Yes, a bar that looks like an abandoned building outside. With no camera in sight." I say finally looking at her,

" Very observant of you, your highness." She says with a roll of her eyes.

I grab her chin between my thumb and forefinger and look in her eyes,

" Don't roll your eyes at me Lei, it was cute the first time but do that again and I will have you bent over my legs with your ass in the air for all to see."

She sucks in a breath, her eyes widening.

" We don't want that, do we Lei?" I ask her. She shakes her head, looking at me.

My cock hardens and I let go of her chin. Walking around with a hard on is not something I plan on doing tonight.

" You called me Lei." She says looking at me,

" Yes, is that not ok?" I ask,

" Well it's ok it's just that you always call me Adair so it is a bit of a shock is all." ,

" I heard your friend call you that and I like it so figured I could use it." I tell her. She nods and looks away,looking back at the dance floor.

" To answer your earlier question, this bar doesn't really have a name. It's just a plus where royal guards come to unwind, we wear masks so no one knows who anyone is, after the stress of being guards, we just like to let loose."

I looked around the room, now seen the people in it in a different way.

" Would they appreciate my being here?" I ask,

" No but then who's going to tell them?" Adair says with a smile. She stands up and takes my hands,

" Dance with me." She tries to pull me to my feet but I don't budge,

" I don't dance." I say simply:

" Please, you didn't come here to sit and watch people." She says still trying to get me to stand up.

" Nope, I find that I like sitting right here and watching people." She let's go if my hands,

" Fine but I am going to dance." She says before turning and walking towards the dance floor. I watch her go because I really just want to go sit and watch her.

Chapter 8

Edward Vaughn

I remain seated and watch Adair go on the dance floor.

The DJ starts playing a fast song and I just sit and watch her.

She's dancing like a dream, moving her body to the rhythm of the beat and she's not holding back. She lifts her hands at some point and her shirt goes up and I see the underside of her breasts. I start getting hard and I try to sit more comfortably to accommodate the growing erection I am having.

Adair looks over her shoulder at me as she dances, her body free. She is enjoying herself, something I can tell from the smile on her face.

" *Come and dance with me.*" She says in my head and I shake my head no. She shrugs and continues dancing.

Someone goes to dance and stands in front of her,blocking my view of her. It isn't until she turns around that I realise that she's dancing with the fucker.

He has his hands around her waist,where my hands had been earlier and I fucking lose it.

I walk to the dance floor and pull Adair out of his hands and straight into mine.

The fucker looks like he wants to argue but one look at my face and he walks away.

Adaid looks at me and smirks,

" You don't want to dance so I got another dance partner who you have now scared away." She's still dancing and I am just standing and holding her waist as if trying to erase the memory of another man's hands on her.

" He had his hands on you." I say in a way of explanation,

" So do you right now." She counters,

" But with ms it's different." I say frustrated,

" Really how so?" Adair has her hands on my shoulders now and is trying to move my body.

" Well it's me and you. You know me but you didn't know that fucker." She laughs shaking her head,

" Actually I knew that 'fucker', his name is Derek. Vaughn you don't own me." I start moving my body mostly so I can feel her against me when she moves.

" I do own you Lei, at least for the next six weeks I do." I tell her with a smirk,

" Ha, keep telling yourself that. I cannot be owned, Vaughn." I pull her closer when a slower song starts playing,

" Lei, I do own you." She stands on toes and kisses me,

" Shut up and dance with me, Vaughn." She kisses me one last time before standing back properly and starts dancing.

She continues dancing like before and I move stiffly with her. I can tell she likes dancing from the way she moves freely and is happy with me.

" You're holding back." She tells me whispering in my ears so I can hear her over the music.

" No, I am not," she almost rolls her eyes at me but stops herself,

" Yes you're. No one here knows who you are and they don't care about you right now. They are here to have fun and listen up after a long day at work so please stop holding back and dance with me."

I look around the dancefloor and the bar and notice no one is looking at us once as we dance.

Another song starts playing and jumps a little, excited

" I love this song." She whispers in my ears.

She removes my hands from her waist and moves through the throng of people dancing around us to go to the centre of the dance floor.

She starts dancing and I stand and watch her. The other dancers leave space for her to dance and start watching her. She dances like a woman on a mission to punish me. Like her body isn't her own any more but is now one with the music and I watch her like a glutton for punishment.

My cock hardens at the sight of her dancing. I have no control over it and I don't care.

It's like she's dancing for me alone and everyone else simply fades in the background, a fire would start and the bloody world would end but I wouldn't leave, I would go down with the fucking building if it meant I got to watch her dance all night long.

All too soon the song ends and people around start clapping for her. She does a little bow before heading over to me. Another song starts playing and people go back to doing their own thing. This time around she doesn't have to beg me to dance with her because I pull her in my arms and she laughs.

" Look who's now ready to dance." Her voice says in my head and she has a smirk on her face.

" Oh you have no idea how much I want to dance with you right now." I whisper in her ear. She simply laughs and continues dancing.

We dance for a long time until I feel my legs start to give out beneath me. I am so fucking hard from all the skin contact and touching we have done but I would die of blue balls a happy man if it means the smile on Adair's face is permanent.

After what seems like hours, we both leave the dance floor and immediately start going out of the bar.

Adair is a little tipsy on her feet from all the drinks she had so I have to hold so she does fall. I nod at Reginald on my way out who nods back.

" You, your highness, are a good dancer." She says smiling.

" Thank you but how about we talk about my dance skills when we are back home." She giggles.

We reach her bike and I start cursing myself. How ths fuck am I

suppose to ride with her when she's clearly tipsy.
" Fuck." I mutter,
" What?" Adair asks me,
" Nothing Lei, come on let me help you wear your helmet." I say instead.
I help her wear her helmet then lift her,
" Wrap your legs around my waist." I tell her.
She does as I tell her.
" How will you ride with me wrapped around you?" She asks me, her voice curious.
" Not sure Lei, we will make it work."
I get on the bike which makes her sit in front of me. A very impractical position if you ask me but one that is necessary at the moment.
" Don't let go." I tell her, starting the engine of the bike,
" I don't think I would if you paid me." She answers, her pussy slightly grazing my still very hard cock. I can feel her heart with layers of clothes between us and stifle a groan.
" Please don't move like that," I all but plead because if she does this with us parked and not moving, I don't think we will make it back to the castle.
" Am sorry I can't help it, I can feel your cock,which by the way is big and hard I haven't seen it but what I have felt today when dancing I know I won't be disappointed," I choke on my saliva but she continues un interpreted,
" And it's pressed against me in the most delicious way plus the vibrations of the bike, fuck I might come from just sitting here."
My cock twitches in my jeans, excited at the prospect of her coming right now.
" How about we ride silently, no talking, ok?" I say not waiting for a reply.
I ride the bike and get us out of the parking lot before I do something I will regret.
Unlike before I don't go the whole ride looking at sights, I spend the whole fucking ride trying not fuck Adair on a moving motorcycle and she doesn't make it any bloody easy.

Her breasts are pressed up against my chest in the most amazing way, her hard nipples not hidden in the slightest by the tiny shirt she wore.
" Oh shit," she says after being quiet for the whole ride.
" You can't ride in, you're sleeping, remember and as much as the guards back at your house respect me, not all of them like me, Donavan will know I left with you without the proper security."
Fuck, after the night I have had all I want to do is go and showed to get rid of the erection I have had for the whole fucking night. I make a right turn into the forests,
" What are you doing? Why are you turning?" She asks,
" You just said I can't go in like this, I think that is bullshit and had you been anyone else I wouldn't have cared because I am the prince of this fucking land but since it's you, well i like you enough to care." I say, parking and turning off the bike when we are a safe distance from the road.
I pull Adair against my erection, making her ride me before I get off the bike,
" Fuckkk, Vaughn." She moans out my name and I swear I get harder. She locks her legs tightly around me when I try to get off the back and rubs her hot core against me once more. I groan and tighten my grip on her to stop her from moving,
" Please don't do that," I all but plead with her again.
" Why not? You are just from doing it." She says still rubbing herself against me. Though the perfect term for what she is doing would be dry humping not that I care because it feels so fucking good.
" I did it to feel you one last time," I say groaning. She takes off her helmet and starts to nibble on my ear lobe,
" Leilani." I growl but I make no move to stop her.
I feel hands moving between us and grab them both pulling them behind her back, I grip both of her hands behind her back,
" Lei, love don't start something you won't be able to finish." I all but growl, my balls blue and aching,
" What makes you think I am not willing to finish?" She ask me looking at me through hooded eyes,

" I know you can finish if we start but I am not about to take advantage of you. You're tipsy, when I have you, I want you sober and awake so you know who is fucking you, who is making you come. When you come it will be with your pussy stuffed full with my cock and on a bed not on top of a motorcycle in a forest off the road." She nods slowly, letting her legs drop to the side,
" Shit shit shit." She says suddenly, her eyes shut as if in pain,
" What's wrong?" I ask,
" Nothing, my leg just brushed the engine. I think I burnt myself." She answers with a little shrug.
I get off the bike and kneel beside her leg, looking at her injured leg,
" Don't worry I will survive,besides I have had worse." She says trying to pull her leg out of my grasp,
" That was before you met, just sit still and let me look at it."
She winces when my fingers touch the burnt area. The good part is it isn't that much of a burn but she will still need aid.
I cover both my hands over the burn and close my eyes.
It doesn't take long for me to feel the power of my gift flowing through me especially since I am in a forest and one one with nature.
My hands start to glow, producing the light of fireflies and I heal her. The pain and burn are all going away.
" You know what, sometimes I forget who you are and then you do things like that and I remember who you are." She says, her voice filled with awe.
" Thank you." I stand up and drop a quick kiss on her forehead,
" You don't need to thank me."
I turn on my gift of imperceptibility again and climb on the bike behind her.
We ride the rest of the way in silence until we get back home. The guards nod to Adair when they see her enter. We pass security all the way to our suite and all they see is her throughout.
She dismisses the guard who stood guarding my empty rooms when we get back and closes the door behind. I turn back to normal and start walking towards my room before stopping and

walking back towards her.
" Thank you for tonight. I had a lot of fun." I say, leaning down and kissing her.
The kiss is supposed to be a brush of lips but we are soon clawing at each other's clothes trying to get each other naked.
Her tongue is in my mouth and I love the taste of her, there's a faint taste of all the spirits she had been drinking tonight.
Gathering all the strength I can find, which is very little because I am hanging by a thread. I push her away and take a step back.
" Good night Lei." I don't bother waiting for a reply. I simply go to my room and lock the door behind me. Fuck I need a shower.

Chapter 9

Edward Vaughn

After my shower and the quickest orgasm my hand has ever given me I go to sleep.
Sleep doesn't come easy and after tossing and turning for hours I give up on the pretense of sleeping and go out for a walk. There's still guards scattered around the house and I start wondering if they ever sleep. I head to the kitchen and grab a bottle of water and I am sure I give a maid there a small heart attack when she sees me in the middle of night in the kitchen.
A few guards fall in step a safe distance away from me when I go out for a walk. The night air is cool and calming, exactly what I need after the evening I have had.
The sound of water waves from the sea hitting the rocks can be heard from where I am standing and I decide to walk to the shores.
The sea looks beautiful at night. I sit on one of the rocks and just relax. Letting my guard down.

∞∞∞

" Good morning Edward." Marshall greets me in the morning during breakfast. I haven't seen much of him in a while because he is always gone or I am too busy.
" Good morning." I answer him.
" Did you just smile?" He asks me like we are teenagers again and something unbelievable has happened.
" Yes, is that a problem?" I ask sarcastically,

" Oh my lord did you get laid or something. You just smiled and made a joke, a sarcastic one yes but still a joke." He asks me, he sounds happy like the matter of my sex life is interesting. I don't answer him though, I simply ignore him and start putting butter on my slice of toast.
" Good morning Marshall, Vaughn." Adair greets us when she enters the room.
She comes to sit next to me and I breathe in her scent that has been a source of comfort for me in the last few days.
Marshall coughs and looks away from Adaur to look at him only to find him laughing.
" You're so fucked." He whispers like a schoolgirl.
I flip him off and ignore him. Adair makes herself a cup of coffee and gets my piece of toast, eating it.
I get another one and start putting butter on it.
" I trust you slept well." I ask her.
" I did," she answers before taking a bite of her toast.
" Left wanting but still had a good night's sleep." Her voice says in my head.
I glare at her before I continue buttering my toast. Marshall abruptly stands and comes over, pulls Adair to her feet and hugs her.
" Thank you." He tells her.
Marshall is a joker half the time but he looks serious right now.
" Why are you thanking me?" Adair asks him, laughing awkwardly,
" Whatever it is you're doing for him, don't stop please. He needs this." He answers. He turns to leave but stops and whispers,
" Don't fuck this up." In my ears and he's gone.
" That was weird." Adair says, sitting back down.
I don't say anything as we sit and eat the rest of our breakfast together.
" What are you doing today?" I find myself asking.
" Whatever you're doing, or have you forgotten that you and I are stuck together." She is looking at me above her mug of coffee,
" Okay then. You and I are going out today. Wear something

light."
I tell her, " We will leave in a few minutes."

∞∞∞

" Where are we going?" Adair asks for the seventh time since we got in the car fifteen minutes ago.
She's wearing a short white dress with flowers on it and has sunglasses covering her eyes.
" You will know when we get there." I answer her.
I got the idea to go out and spend the day on my watch at sea today. I was going to be alone but then I changed my mind when I saw Adair today.
Ambrosia is an island surrounded by seas meaning there are a lot of harbours but we are going to the royal harbour because it's private and safer.
I make a right turn and start driving down a private road that leads to the harbour.
" Yes! I finally got it." She says looking at me, " We are going to the royal harbour."
I smile but say nothing. I want to relax and I want to relax with her. I just hope she likes what I have planned.
" Fine, I wait patiently and see what you have planned but now I know it's at the harbour."
I drive in silence until arrive at the harbour.
Someone comes to open my door and I immediately go around to open the door for Adair.
" Thank you." She says when I offer my hand.
" Welcome your highness. Everything is ready for you." The captain tells me with a smile on his face.
" Thank you very much." I answer him.
Adair is looking around at the yachts docked.
" Let's go." I tell Adair.
She walks beside me, a little nervous. We go to the yacht that is

docked the furthest.
" Elspeth?" She asks me, reading the names on the yacht.
" After mom." I reply.
" I know who she is. I am just shocked you named it after, is all." She tells me with a nervous smile.
I internally slap myself, of course she knows who it is, I may have lost my mother but the kingdom lost a queen.
" Come on,let's board. We are wasting time standing here and simply staring at it." I say pushing her towards the ramp.
" Let me give you a tour." I say when we are on board.
" Please, lead the way."
I take pride in Elspeth. Father has about six yachts or maybe more but I only have one. Where his are a big fuck you to everyone I have mine because I love been at sea.
Mom bought it for me when I turned twelve and we would come out to paint the sea and the animals.
I haven't been on Elspeth since mom's death. I feel lighter coming back here like I am slowly facing all my demons head on and I have Adair to thank for that.
I show around, leaving the best for last.
" This is beautiful,did you paint it?" She asks me, referring to a dolphin I painted when I was thirteen.
" Thank you. It was my first time painting and drawing a living breathing thing so it meant a lot." I answer with a smile. I forgot about it. I remember when I finished painting it, mom finally agreed to sit still so I could paint her because she had been refusing up until then. Her reasoning being that why should she sit still for hours only to come out looking horrible. I laugh a little at the memory.
Adair gently touches my shoulder as if aware about the route my memory had taken me.
" Come on, I saved the best part for last and I can only show it to you when we are out on the ocean and not docked." She looks at me skeptical,
" And how do you intend to do that?" She asks,
" You will see but you have to trust me." I tell her, holding up a

blind fold.

" I am doing this because I am genuinely curious but if you do something shitty Vaughn I will slowly break all the bones in your body, wait for you to heal then do it all over again." I shudder,

" What scares me the most about your statement is the fact that you can go through with it but don't worry, I won't do anything you won't like."

She lets me blind fold her then I guide her to a bedroom.

" Stay here, I will come and get you once I have sailed us to the perfect spot." I tell dropping a quick kiss on her forehead.

" You can take off your blind fold in here but only if you promise to stay here and not come up." I tell her before leaving.

I go to the upper deck and sail away from the dock.

After fifteen minutes I finally dock where I feel comfortable we will be alone. Not a single soul to disturb us for miles and most important not a single guard or pesky security.

I set up Adair's surprise before going below deck to get her.

" Sorry it took some time." I say opening the door.

I find her sleeping where I left her with the blind fold still on and the sight makes my cock twitch a little from his resting place. Down boy, we are here to relax and nothing more.

" I started dozing, good thing you came back when you did." She answers me standing up. " Can I take the blind off now."

" Yes, sorry I got distracted. Come on, let's go." I tell her.

She takes the blind fold off and I lead her above deck to her surprise.

She gasps when she finds the setup I did for her.

" Vaughn wow," she says, going to kneel down and picking up one of the books.

I had ordered some novels for her after seeing the one she had been reading in the gym last time. I don't know what half the books are about but I figured she would like them plus what better way to read than on a yacht underneath the warm sun.

" How did you get these,Vaughn? Some of these aren't even set to release until next year." She looks so damn happy that I know it is worth all that time I spent reading reviews of authors just so I could know which book to get her.

" Thank you so much, no one has ever done something like this for me." She says standing up and coming to hug me.

" I am glad you like it. I also got you a bottle of wine and grapes. I have seen how much you like them." I say teasing.

" Seriously Vaughn, thank you. A glass of wine does sound lovely right now." She tells me, smiling.

" Go and sit over there and read your book. I will bring you your wine and grapes. You are always taking care of me, today I am your servant." I tell her.

I go below deck to get two glasses of wine and grapes for her. When I go back up, I find she has set a blank canvas for me and some paint.

" It's only fair that you relax while I relax. Besides you're my servant today, your words not mine so I command you to relax and paint." She tells me getting the wine glass and platter of grapes from my hands.

She doesn't wait for a reply but goes and grabs a book from the library I had built for her. She sets them all beside a towel she has sores on the deck.

I watch her transfixed as she strips off her dress, pulling it over her head and leaving her in a pair of blue lace panties. And her breasts, lord. A better man would look away but I am not a better man and I never said I was so I stare at her. My cock grows hard but I ignore it now as I stare at her.

" Staring is rude." Her voice says in my head,

" At this point I am happy being rude if it means I get to look at you." I answer her with a dry chuckle.

She laughs at my reply but says nothing. She puts on her sunglasses and lays down on her stomach then proceeds to read her book.

I chug my glass of wine and go back to get myself the whole bottle because I have a feeling I will be needing a lot of wine today.

∞∞∞

After taking a nap, I wake up and find Adair still reading her book. The only thing that has changed since before my nap is her sleeping position. She is now laying her back, her breasts on full display for anyone to see.
Thank fuck there's no one near us for miles because i don't want any other man looking at her the way she is right now.
I stare at the blank canvas she brought for me and decide, what the heck I will try to paint.
I get a stool and a pencil then look at my inspiration.
I start to draw her, how I see her. The first few minutes into drawing her it's just me roughly shading to see how things will go, if at all I'll be able to draw or paint.
After a few minutes, I notice that I am not struggling and draw with a little more purpose now.
I capture her,not just how she looks but the scene around her as well. I capture her emotion, her carefree nature and the smiles that keep appearing on her face when she reads something naughty in her book. I capture not just the woman but the emotion she brings and I feel emotion I haven't felt in a while swell in me. I stop looking at her when I am done drawing her and look at the canvas. My heart swells with something you can't name and the emotion is so great I almost choke.
" Your eyes have changed again." Leilani says and I look up to find her standing in front of me.
" I am sorry, they do that sometimes." I answer her with my voice full of emotion.
" You're crying." It's a statement not a question. I wipe my cheeks and my hands come back wet with tears.
" I guess I am." She comes to stand behind me, to look at my drawing of her.
" Wow, you're amazing. Vaughn, this looks beautiful." She says

once she's seen the painting.
" Why are you crying, I thought maybe the drawing was bad." She tells me, trying to make a joke of it with a little laugh.
" I haven't drawn or painted anything since mom died. This is the first time I have painted without any hindrance. This is the first time I have drawn without my mind freezing up Lei." My voice is so full of emotion that I don't even recognize it myself.
Leilani doesn't say anything for a few minutes,she just stands behind me and lets me take it all in.
" Well I am glad me and my boobs could help you." She jokes after some time.
" They really have been a source of inspiration, haven't they." I answer her, laughing.
" I have never met anyone like you, Lei." I say after a while.
" I have never met anyone like me either." She admits with a shrug.
" Remember what I told you last night." She doesn't answer me but I know she remembers when her cheeks pinken.
" You are a unique person, Lei. You have been half naked in front of me for the last six hours, reading about lord knows what but if it's anything like what I found you reading in the gym then it's some good nasty stuff but I remind you of my promise last night and you blush." I tell her, pulling her to stand between my spread legs.
This position makes my head at the same level as the breasts I have been staring at for the better part of the day.
" I am very comfortable in my nakedness. Besides I didn't pack a bikini and I inspired you so it is a win-win situation." She answers me.
I pull one of her breasts in my mouth and suck on it. She gasps softly, her hands going to my head and holding me against her breast.
I stop sucking on her breast and look at her instead.
" Last night I said I wanted you on my bed but I have changed my mind." I tell her, one of my hands is playing with the lace of her panties.

" I want you out here on the deck. Under the sun so I can see you and worship you like you deserve to be worshipped. Nothing about this will be quick Lei, I want you to come so many fucking times that you won't be able to walk straight for days."
She moans at my words. I take off her sunglasses.
" When I fuck you I want to be able to see your eyes." I say kissing her.
Our kiss is passionate and fierce. She wants control and I want control so it's a fight,to see who will give up control for the other.
I kiss her, pulling her tongue in my mouth and sucking on it, my hands landing her soft ass.
My mouth leaves hers and I start kissing a trail down her neck. I kiss and nip on her skin, her neck, her earlobe and she shivers in my hands.
My mouth finds her breasts and I suck on the left one. I suck on it like a man starved and she is my last meal. Leilani moans loudly and holds my head against my chest. I bring my hand to her other breast and mold and tug on her nipple giving both breasts attention.
I stop sucking on her left breast and go to her right breast giving both of them the attention they need.
I stand abruptly and lift Leilani, putting on the stool I had been sitting on.
I spread her legs and go down on my knees ready to worship her.
I take a whiff of her through her panties like an addict and she is my favourite drug.
" Lift your bum a little love." I tell her tugging on her panties. I am surprised I have the patience to remove them because my hands are shivering right now. She does as I tell her and her panties are soon off leaving her gloriously naked before me.
" Hold on to the stool love, when I start, I won't be able to stop." I tell her.
I start kissing her from her belly button going down. I kiss and lick my way down until I find where she craves me the most.
She is so fucking wet and she smells amazing.
" Spread your legs for me love." I tell her, my voice hoarse. She

spreads her legs for me and I pull her towards the edge of the stool then put both her legs on either side of the stool.
I lick her from her ass to her pussy and she moans loudly. I groan at her test and I have a sudden epiphany that I might just get addicted to her, the taste of her.
She uses her fingers to spread her lips for me and I auck on her swollen nub which listens against the sun.
" Don't you dare fucking stop Vaughn." She tells me on another moan. She doesn't have to worry about that, the world would be ending for all I care and I wouldn't stop.
I suck on her clit and bite her a little, making her moan.
I go down further and start fucking her with my tounge while my hands play with her nipple. I suck, fuck and lick her,savouring her because she is the finest meal I have ever had.
She comes on my tongue screaming my name but I don't stop eating her out until she finishes riding her wave.
I stand up and hold her against me. She is a shivering mess and her body might as well be boneless at the moment.
" Wow," Is all she says, I smirk.
She tries to get off the stool but u stop her,
" I didn't say you could get down." I tell her, my fingers going where my tongue had just been.
She moans when I touch her, her pussy swollen and sensitive to my touch.
" Well you better make this one count as well then." She tells me, the cheeky little thing.
" I will." I say against her lips kissing her just as I put my middle finger in her.
She clamps around my finger immediately, her pussy tight. She moans in my mouth and I start moving my finger in her.
She rides it and I and a second one. She moans, burying her face in my neck as I finger her.
I curl my fingers inside her and hitting a spot that makes her scream and I press my thumb on her clit, applying pressure on both sides to make her cum. I hit that spot again and she comes a second time, this time screaming in my ears. My ears hurt from

her screaming but I would do this again if it means she cums screaming my name like there is no tomorrow.
I lift her off the stool and lay her down on her towel, the one she spent her day on reading.
I quickly strip off all my clothes and join her on the towel.
" Your eyes are still red." She tells me as her curious hand grips my cock. I groan loudly almost coming from the contact alone.
" Please stop before I come before the fun begins." I say my voice hoarse.
The little devil doesn't let go, she instead guides my cock to her opening, rubbing me against her.
" Fuck, Lei I will bloody come before the fun begins." I say moving my body against her. Loving the feel of her wet and warm against my cock.
" You're a lot bigger than I am used to." She says and I groan.
" Love no man wants to hear the woman he is about to fuck talk about other men during sex." I say still moving as she rubs ms against her.
" Trust me, I don't even remember what they look like right now." She says.
" Guide me in." I all but beg her.
She guides me to her entrance and I thrust into her and groan at.
" Fuck. You feel so damn good." I say kissing her.
" You feel good, yourself." She says in my mind again.
I start moving and she moans. Fuck.
Leilani not only move s when thrust but gets up to meet ms thrust for thrust. She isn't shy about how she wants me and I give her what she asks for. I love women who aren't afraid to Express the sexual wants or desires and I can safely say Leilani is vocal about what she likes.
" Fuck Vaughn I am going to come." She tells me panting. I angle my cock in a way that I hit her clit every time I thrust and she explodes around me. Clumping around me and I follow her, cuming harder than I ever have in my life.
I collapse on top of her breathing hard.
" That was, wow." She says her voice breathless.

I laugh a little and get off of her, laying down next to her, pulling her into my hands.
" You were amazing." I tell her kissing her head.
We lay still for a few minutes trying to catch our breaths.
" I am going to shower." Lei says standing up. I make a move to follow her but she stops me,
" I meant alone besides we have to be getting back."
" We can shower together and still have enough time to get back, Lei." I tell her.
" No Vaughn, this was nice the sex was amazing but I don't want to go back smelling like sex and looking like I have just been thoroughly fucked."
" But you have been thoroughly fucked, my ears are still ringing from your screaming." I say getting a little frustrated.
" Vaughn please, I have an image to uphold. I don't want to be known as that keeper that fucked the prince when he was engaged to someone else," my eyes widen, i didn't know she knew that.
" Yes, I know you're engaged. I am not saying I regret what happened,far from it. I enjoyed this so much,you're a good man but I have a reputation to uphold. If Donavan finds out about this."
I snap at her when she mentions Donavan's name,
" What the fuck does Donavan have to do with this,with us. Are fucking him?" Her eyes widen ever so slightly and I know I have overstepped.
" Who I fuck or don't fuck isn't your business Vaughn, what i do with my boyfriend isn't your business. You can fuck me when you're engaged and I have to turn the other way but the moment I do it you want to pull the power card on me. Fuck you, your highness." She says, picking up her clothes and going below deck to shower. Fuck I messed up.

Chapter 10

Edward Vaughn

I start sailing us back while Leilani is in the shower. Fuck I messed up.

I haven't felt like this in a while and I have Leilani to thank for that but I messed that up. Fuck.

I don't even refer to her as Adair anymore.

She's finished bathing by the time I dock and she gets off the yacht before me. I go and the drawing I did of her because the thought of another man looking at her the way I did today makes my blood boil.

The sun is setting by the time we get back home following the most silent car ride.

Leilani gets out of the car before again and heads straight to her room.

I look for a room where I can put the drawing where no one can see it and lock the door.

During dinner it's just me and Marshall. He has been glaring at me since I started eating and hasn't said a word but he probably has ahit to say since he keeps looking at me like he wants to kill me.

" Do you have something to say or will you just glare at the through the whole fucking meal?" I ask him.

" No,just wondering how such an intelligent man can be such a damn idiot."

" Explain." I answer, confused.

" I haven't seen you so carefree since knowing you Edward. This morning you looked happy, so fucking happy and carefree and I was happy for you because you can't just go through life been pissed at the world. But you fucked it up, I don't know what you did to her but it's responsible for your dark mood and her not eating so you better apologise to her after dinner."
He gets up taking his plate of food with him.
" Where are you going?" I ask him.
" To the study,I have work to do so I will eat from there."
He leaves after delivering his speech and I find that I no longer have an appetite. I stand and go upstairs to my room, after the day I have had all I want to do is sleep.

I don't know how I got here.
I went to my room to sleep but when I couldn't sleep, I got the urge to paint. I got a blank canvas and some paint brushes and a pencil inorder to do so but I couldn't.
My muse for painting was in the room next to mine, upset with me.
I did the next best thing in my opinion, I teleported to her room with my canvas and paint and pencils and decided to paint her whilst she slept.
I was going to go back to my room but I found I couldn't and I have since been in Leilani's room for the past four hours drawing her while she sleeps.
Creepy yes and I am sure she will have my balls once she wakes up.
She looks beautiful when she sleeps, her hair is like a curtain of brown curls against her pillow.
I discovered that she sleeps completely naked for one when her sheets slipped and showed a creamy thigh and ass.
She felt me when I first came in, I know she did but she

pretended to sleep but her pretense soon gave way to actual sleep.
Her breathing has been going slow and steady for hours and I have been drawing her.
I know it immediately when she wakes up but I say nothing. She turns and looks at me, covering her exposed bum.
" Staring is rude." She says finally looking at me. Her voice sounds scratchy from sleep.
" So I have been told." She sits up, the sheets pooling around her waist.
" What do you want Vaughn, I let you stay here like a creep while you were drawing but I would now like to be alone." She sounds snappy.
" Wrong, you let me stay because you like it when I look at you." I say, telling her the truth.
" Vaughn, what is it you want?" She asks me knowing that arguing is moot.
" I came to apologise. I acted like an ass today, you don't owe me any explanations and I was an ass for assuming that you did." I tell her.
" It's okay, I should have known better than to sleep with you but I did it anyway."
" Am sorry, I should have known better as well because like you said I am engaged. It's just that I am drawn to you. It must be you because you don't even notice it. I am not the only one, your guards, most of them like you, I can read their thoughts and half the time I am controlling myself so I don't kill them. When I am with you, I am at peace and this thing between us Lei ut goes way beyond physical attraction." I tell her.
Even though she's sitting in bed and I am standing behind a canvas, there might as well be nothing between us from all the tension.
" Thank you for listening to me and once again I am sorry. I will leave you to sleep now." I tell her before disappearing and finding myself back in my room.
I look at my new drawings and take them to the room with the

one I had drawn of her earlier today.
Knowing I won't be able to sleep for the rest of the night, I put up the first canvas, the one I drew first and decided to paint it.
I am mixing paint colors to get the exact shade of her eyes when the door suddenly opens and Leilani steps in, closing the door behind her.
She's carrying a plate of cookies and two glasses of milk with her. She says nothing as she comes to sit next to me and sets the tray of food between us.
She's now wearing a robe, thankfully because I can't concentrate with her naked.
The room I am using to store my paintings and drawings of her is more of a closet albeit a large closet so there isn't much space separating us.
She gets a book from her pocket, takes a bite of a cookie and starts reading, ignoring me.
I look at her and smile before I continue mixing my paint.
I munch on a few cookies as I paint and drink my milk and she just sits and reads not saying anything.
Before I know it, I am almost halfway done painting and time has flown by so fast.
My legs start cramping so I stand and stretch them.
Leilani doesn't look up from her book, silent as a mouth. The only noise she has made since joining me is the sound of her turning a page or her faking a bite of a cookie and chewing it.
I sit back down and continue painting but stop when I feel her eyes on. I continue painting.
" Staring is rude." I tell her without looking up from what I am doing.
" You don't say." She answers me, her voice light. " I couldn't sleep." She says after a heartbeat.
" Really, I couldn't tell." My voice is sarcastic and she punches my shoulder.
I try not to wince because it hurts like a bitch, had it been any other woman, I would have thought she was fighting and trying to act cute but with Leilani I know she meant for it to hurt.

" I forgive you, for today. I knew it was going to get messy when I decided to start kissing you but well, I like to flirt with danger."
I put away my paint brush and paint to look at her.
" Thank you." I tell her.
She puts her book down and stands up.
" Well, I am going to work out or sleep. I am not yet sure which it is I will be doing." She tells me, walking towards the door.
" You know, other than word of mouth. I haven't seen you fight or defend yourself." I tell her.
She stops in her tracks and turns around facing me once again.
" Because there hasn't been a need to. When I fight, I fight to kill not to please your curiosity, Vaughn."
I think I have a death wish because that is the only way I can explain what I tell her next.
" Lei, I came into your room and left unscathed. I could have been a threat, I could have killed you." I say with a smirk.
" I let you come into my room, I let you draw me, Vanugh. Keyword been let, had I wanted you could have left with one eye."
She's smiling, enjoying the banter.
" Of course you did, love." My tone is condescending and sarcastic.
Like a flash, I am pinned against the wall and there's a dagger pressed against my throat.
Leilani's eyes flash violet but it happens so fast that I am certain I simply imagined it.
The dagger against my throat moves lower until it pressed against my chest, tight above my heart.
" Don't tempt me. I have become quite fond of you and all your body parts. It would be a shame if you lost some of them."
I swallow, my cock getting hard like a sick psycho.
" Well those body parts must have left such an impression on you then." I tell her with a smirk.
I try to lower my head, to kiss her behind her ear but pressure on the knife against my chest increases.
" Are you simply going to use it as a threat or will you actually do

some damage?" I ask her knowing her knife can't hurt me.
She smiles cheekily and slashes my chest.
I almost scream at the agonising pain.
What the fuck is that?
I have never felt such intense pain in my life, especially considering it's from such a small cut. At Least I think it's a small cut.
I try to look down to see what damage the little minx has caused but the dagger moves from my chest to my throat.
I am now kind of scared of bleeding if she decides to slice open my throat.
" What the fuck is that?" I ask her wincing because my skin feels like it's on fire fro.where she cut me.
She lets go of me and steps back.
" Nothing to worry your pretty little head about love." She says in the same tone I had used on her earlier.
" Vaughn, I am a keeper. You should know I take my job seriously." She tells me before going out of the room.
The fact that she was able to draw blood only makes me hard.
I smile to myself as I feel the cut.
The fucking minx sliced the letter L on my skin, she branded me.
I should be upset but I am not. I will proudly wear this scar.
Nothing has scared or turned me on before but this definitely did.

My body is running on not much sleep apart from the nap I took yesterday on the yacht.
Since I don't have any obligations today, I decided to take Marshall on a tour or rather I found someone to take us on a tour.
I haven't had a free day with him since coming back so spending today with him is a must.
He came to visit and I am either busy or tired.

Leilani isn't part of my security today, so it's just Reginald and some other guards whose names I don't know.

I am waiting in the car for Marshall to come out but he is taking forever.

The door opens and he steps inside,

" Good morning. Sorry I took so long, I couldn't decide what to wear, I am just so excited for our date." She says smiling like a loon.

Reginald looks behind with a weird expression on his face. I roll my eyes.

Marshall has always had a weird sense of humor,so every now and then he thinks it's a good idea to pretend that I am gay and I secretly love him but I can't do shit about it.

He means nothing offensive by it, he just enjoys fucking with me.

He looks over at Reginald and laughs noticing his expression.

" Wow, these guys are easy to rile. Seriously though, sorry it took time. I had to write something down before I forget about it." He says fastening his seat belt.

Marshall is intelligent, very intelligent but he is also very forgetful.

He will have this amazing idea that can change the world in one minute and then forget it in the next. Because of that,he has taken to walking around with a journal.

Mona, his younger sister calls it his diary, something that pisses him off but I guess that the whole point of her calling it a diary.

" It's ok. Was it important?" I ask him as the driver drives out of the yard.

" No, but I just had to write it down." I simply nod.

The drive to the city is quiet with Marshall on his phone all the way and me trying my hardest not to think about Leilani.

I manage for the most part but then the mark on my chest itches and I try not to smile.
When we get to the city, we are introduced to our guide for the day. A chirpy college kid who is so nervous that I am surprised she doesn't throw up.
She is in awe, her thoughts tell me that much but she also wants to make a good impression, not just because I am the prince but because she also wants a good grade from doing this tour.
I smile internally. I never really had to worry about my grades in school. Mostly because I was good at everything but also because all the schools I attended were afraid of angering father.
He thinks I don't know about this but I do, I could understand the teachers thoughts after all.
We spend the rest of the day going around the city.
Ambrosia really is a great kingdom. All its inhabitants do well, free education and free health care throughout the kingdom and I couldn't be more proud.
Businesses are booming and there's employment for everyone.
Which is why when I become king, I will be putting all my energy into making the small independent islands surrounding Ambrosia as great as Ambrosia.
Father doesn't do shit for them because in his words 'they are not our problem' something I think is bullshit.
I have been to those islands and seen the suffering, the hunger, the lack of healthcare and what not.
I may not have any experience ruling but one thing is for sure, I will not be the same king my father and grandfather have been in the past.

After hours of exploring, I ask Reginald to find us a place to eat with good food because I am starving and I am sure they are as well.

He takes over driving duties and takes us to a restaurant by the seaside.
It's empty except for a few servers and two chefs who are all out front to greet me.
" Welcome, your highness." They all greet me, bowing, " Mr Thatcher." The waitress says, referring to Marshall who nods a greeting in return.
" We are honoured to have you, please where would you like to sit." She asks us.
Reginald and some other guards do a sweep of the place and nod so me and Marshall go and sit at the table in the corner of the room. Hidden from everyone's eyesight.
The other waitress brings out the menus for us and we order.
She brings me water and a bottle of wine for Marshall.
I take a sip of my water and Marshall pours himself a glass of wine.
" I wanted to see the city but damn am I tired." Marshall says after drinking the full glass of wine on one go.
" You never exercise so this was a good way to burn some fat." I tell him.
He doesn't answer me for a few minutes, simply staring at me.
" She's good for you." He says after some time.
" Who?" I ask him playing dumb.
" Leilani. I don't know what she did but I have noticed you especially when you think I am not looking, Edward you look lighter. Happier. She has done for you what I have been unable to do since knowing you."
He waits for me to say something but when I say nothing he drops the topic.
Our food is soon served and we eat with an easy conversation.
Marshall has a lot to say, I know because I can hear it all but he says nothing.
I appreciate his silence because I don't even know what is happening with Leilani. When I am ready I will tell him about it but for now, I want to figure things out myself.

Chapter 11

Edward Vaughn

When we get back home at 7PM. Marshall goes straight to shower and I go to my room.
I don't find Leilani in her room so I head to the gym and find her lifting dumbbells that look like they could crush her if she somehow dropped them but she lifts them with so much ease.
I enter quietly, taking off my shoes and shirt leaving me only in jeans.
I take off my wrist watch as well and walk slowly towards her. She is listening to music using headphones so I don't think she hears me.
I wait for her to put the dumbbells down before sneaking up and lifting her off her feet.
She laughs like a child,carefree and happy.
" Fuck, Vaughn put me down." She's still laughing.
I put her down and she turns around to face me.
" That was sneaky." She says, trying to catch her breath.
" Really, isn't that exactly what you did this morning?"
She smirks when I mention what happened this morning and looks at my chest, looking at the mark.
" Really Vaughn. So like a man to not accept that a woman can beat them at something."
She's baiting me, I know she is. I mean she is a keeper, not like the ancient keepers but a modern keeper nevertheless so she has to be a good fighter and strong as well but I am stranger than her.

" Lei, I can beat you. I could kick box you right now but I would think of other interesting things to do that involve less blood and bodily harm."
I tell her, eying her little shorts and tiny shirt.
" Wow. Ok how about we make a deal, one round of kickboxing, I beat you and you tell me about your mom because you never talk about her and if you beat me, I am yours for a day."
I stop and think. It's true, I never talk about mom unless it's necessary. We have been stuck together at the hip since I came back and I know more shit about her than she does about me so I know how curious she must be. Plus me winning and having her for the whole day has a lot of advantages.
" Ok, but when I beat you, you won't need underwear for the whole fucking day."
" So confident, your highness. Bare knuckle, I hate the gloves."
She says looking serious. Whenever she calls me your highness, I hate it because it reminds me of everything we seem to forget when we're together but when she calls me your highness like she just did, it turns me on.
I haven't fought bare knuckle with someone in a long time, I used to with Marshall but we stopped and started using boxing gloves after I broke his nose.
We move to the boxing ring in the gym, she gets in first and I watch her move around, stretching.
I get in after her, and start to take off my jeans.
" What are you doing?" She asks me, her voice going high.
" My movements will be restricted if I fight in jeans. Don't worry I am fighting in my boxer briefs." I tell her with a smirk.
She nods and stands in the middle of the ring. I grow my jeans out and stand in front of her.
" Bring everything you've got Lei, I'll fight dirty." I say shaking her hand.
" So will I."
She steps back and we start to circle each other.
I won't be using my strength because I don't want to harm her in any way.

Being the gentleman I am,I wait for her to take the first swing at me, so that you know it's fair.
She throws and lands her punch on my left cheek and I swear I hear bones snap.
I find myself on my ass, knocked out with one swing.
" I win." She says, gloating.
" No, I want a rematch, I wasn't ready."
She laughs but nods her head. I stand up, feeling my cheek to make sure it's still there because fuck, she's a puncher.
What the fuck do they feed them.
This time around, I am ready for her. We start to circle each other again.
I throw a punch, which she dodges and she punches me again,my right cheek this time and like the first time around, I end up on my ass.
" Would you like another rematch? Your highness." She's smiling like the cat that got the mouse.
I am breathing hard from the pain, it might be temporary but it still hurts like a bitch.
She offers me her hand and I take it and she helps me get up.
" I could take you up on your rematch but I am sure the end result will be as embarrassing as the last two matches. Well played Lei." I say pulling her close to me.
" Don't worry, atleast was here to witness your embarrassment."
She stands on her tiptoes and kisses me on both cheeks,
" I am sorry but well I hate being underestimated." She tells me, looking me in the eyes.
She stands back on her feet but I pull her against me and lift her, wrapping her legs around my waist.
" I promise to never underestimate you again." I say against her lips.
I feel her smile against my lips and gently bite her lower lip.
She kisses me, wrapping her hands around my neck.
I let her take the lead and kiss me but I soon take over.
My hands knead her ass and she sighs in my mouth. I take the opportunity to slip my tongue into her mouth and she sucks on

it.
I am now fully hard and almost come from that alone.
" I know I am immortal but fuck it, Leilani you will be the death of me." I say against her lips.
She starts grinding her wet core against me and I groan.
She's already wet and ready, I can feel her through her shorts.
Without stopping kissing her, I walk us to the corner of the boxing ring and sit down with her in my lap.
The new position puts her in direct contact with my cock and she grinds against it,both of us moaning from contact.
One of my hands moves between us, slipping inside her little shorts until I find her core. Wet,hot and ready for me.
I put two of my fingers inside her and she moans loudly.
I start to fuck her with my fingers and she moves against my hand,riding it. I feel her start to tighten against my hand, about to explode.
" Edward." I hear father's voice outside the gym door.
" Fuck fuck fuck." Leilani says, trying to stand up. I pull her back down.
" I am not going to leave you hanging, let me finish what I started." I whisper in her ear.
My fingers start moving again,
" Vaughn please, your father is outside the door. What if he comes in?" She says, breathing hard.
She tries to stop her body from moving against mine, tries to stop her body's response but in the past few days,I have come to know her body better than I know my own.
I find the spot that makes her lose her mind and add pressure on it. She almost screams, a sound I manage to stop with a kiss.
" Are you sure he is in there?" I hear father ask someone in the corridors.
The old man has always had bad timing.
" If your father comes in here and finds me riding your fingers, I will cut them all off." Lei says in my head.
She's still riding my fingers, tightening around them.
Someone starts to break the door down, at father's request but I

don't stop.
Lei comes and the door breaks open but no one sees us because I teleport us out at that very moment.
Her eyes are closed and she's shaking from the orgasm and adrenaline surge she just felt.
She opens her eyes when she stops hearing voices and finds herself in the living outside our bedrooms upstairs.
" Fuck I forgot you could do that." She says, her breath still shallow.
I take her to her room and put her on the bed.
" This isn't finished, I am coming back but let me see what father wants."
I tell her before leaving the room. I close the door behind me and go to my room.
No sooner have I put on a pair of sweatpants that my bedroom door opens and father walks in, followed closely by Donavan.
" Where the hell have you been? I have been looking for you." She asks me in an angry voice.
" It's late, I was obviously in my room."
He looks at me skeptical. I already know I look like a mess. My hair is messed up from Leilani running her fingers through it, my lips are probably swollen from the kissing but I have to give father credit because he says nothing.
" Get presentable and meet me in the parking lot, I want to talk to you." He tells me before leaving.
Fuck, that definitely killed my erection.

I go out to the parking lot after getting dressed and find father waiting for me.
" Walk with me." He tells me when he sees me approaching him.
I walk beside him and we walk away from the cars and all his security. I notice Donavan is no longer with him but say nothing for the most part.
His visit today is unexpected and out of the blue so I am genuinely curious as to what made him come all the way here to see me.

" Edward, I have been keeping track of you. Nothing disrespectful but I just wanted to make sure you're okay and that you're not being followed."
I almost roll my eyes. How is having someone followed respectful. I hold my tongue instead.
" I understand the temptation you must have faced, Leilani Adair is an attractive young lady but she is a keeper. We never ever get involved with her kind."
I look at him, surprised that he knows about me and Lei.
" Yes I know," he says after seeing my shocked expression.
" You know all this happened behind closed doors and not in public, I wouldn't have had a problem with it but Esward you took her out at the royal dock. You do realise that your marriage to Madison is all but final. We are strengthening our kingdoms here. Boy, I thought you wanted what is best for Ambrosia and its people." I say nothing, simply listen.
" How am I supposed to abdicate when you think with the brain between your legs and not the one above your shoulders. I understand that this is all a ruse to distract the media and for your safety but I didn't expect you to take it seriously. End things and keep your relationship with her professional immediately. Am I understood?" He asks me.
" Yes father." I say.
He nods and turns around, walking back towards the cars. I walk beside him and help him get into the car before going back inside.
I have never disobeyed father. His word is gold, what he wants me to do but for the first time I know I won't let Lei go because what I feel for this woman goes way beyond physical attraction.
The corridors are empty of any guards which is very much out of the ordinary but I don't think anything of it until I am a few feet from the door to my private living room, the one that leads to me and Lei's rooms.
I hear Donavan's voice first.
" You had one assignment, you where nit supposed to fuck him. I thought you were above that, I thought you took your job

seriously. I didn't expect you to fuck him."

My hands are folded into fists, it's all I can do to stop myself from beating Donavan black and blue for his disrespectful comments.

" I take my job seriously, you of all people should know that. Who I fuck or don't fuck isn't any if your business Donavan, we are not exclusive, I can sleep with the whole damn royal guard and you wouldn't so shit because you don't own me." Leilani answers him, her voice furious.

Internally, I clap for her, for standing up for herself not for threatening to sleep with the whole royal guard. That part has me wanting to spank her.

I walk in on them and Donavan bows from waist down though he would rather stab me.

" I am sorry your highness, I didn't mean to come to your private rooms." I give a flick of my fingers and he stands up to his full height.

" You know Donavan, I would throw my weight and title around. Shove my crown up your ass and threaten you, but I won't do any of that because I know that she," I say pointing at Lei, who still looks deliciously bedraggled,

" Can take care of herself. Do not interfere in her work or punish her in any way. You don't want to see me angry."

I make my eyes change colors on purpose and my long claws come out.

Donavan is no fool, he looks scared shitless and ready to.run but he stands waiting for me to dismiss him.

" Understood, your highness." He all but spits.

" You're dismissed, I am sure father is waiting for you."

He leaves quickly and I know he won't tell father a word about what happened here.

I lock the door behind him before returning to face Leilani.

" I am sorry about that." I say, going to take a seat on the couch.

" Why, you did me a favour, anyway I have gone to sleep. It's late and this has been a very eventful evening."

She comes and kisses ms softly before going to her room.

" You owe me."

I smile at her voice in my head. Fuck this woman will be the death of me.

Chapter 12

Edward Vaughn

I wake up to consistent knocking on my door.

I open the door to find Leilani dressed in black jeans, riding boots and a black riding jacket.

" Good morning Vaughn." She greets me in a sunny and happy voice.

I don't answer her but I leave my door open so she can enter behind me.

I hear the faint click of the door, my confirmation that the door is locked behind me.

" Why aren't you in the gym?" I ask her from my bathroom.

I start brushing my teeth and don't bother shaving my morning shadow.

" I figured I would go riding and since I knocked to the ground not once but twice last night and you owe me your story, I thought what the heck, you can come along as well."

Of course she did. I try not to smile because I am happy spending time with her anyway I can, even if it means I have to stop about my past.

I take off my pajamas and wear a towel around my waist before going to my walk-in closet, which can be accessed through my room.

Leilani is laying on my bed with her boots on the ground. Her mouth opens slightly when she sees me and I smirk.

" Staring is rude." I say her in the same no nonsense tone she uses

when she tells me that.
" With views like this, I can understand why you stare." She answers me laughing.
I find a section of clothes that are specifically reserved for riding and get a pair of trousers from there and a pair of boots and a riding jacket.
The trousers look so fucking tight that for the moment I am scared for my balls but when I wear them, I discover they are quite comfortable.
I go out when I am done dressing and find Leilani playing with the little dagger she used on me. She puts it away when she sees me and gets up from the bed.
" If I had known riding would mean you wear those trousers and showcase your ass, I would have suggested we go riding sooner." She teases.
" Only for you. I don't like riding." I tell her as we walk out of my room.
A few guards bow when they see me but I don't pay them any attention.
" Really? Then what's with all the horses?"
Marshall asked me the same exact thing when he found out I bought horses.
" Mom liked riding. She liked the outdoors, she loved nature so I keep the horses in memory of her." I answer her.
We are now outside the house but it's a few minutes walk to the stable.
" I understand that but Vaughn, you have a stable with a hundred plus horses."
She makes a good point. What no one but my stable master knows is that, about seventy of the horses I bought were going to be killed because they're too old so I bought them. I think only a dozen or two dozen of the horses in my stables can be used for riding.
" Well, I have more than enough money." I answer her instead.
We walk in silence for a few minutes, the only noise being made is the sound of our boots against the pavements as we walk.

There are two guards walking behind us but they are too far away to hear anything we are saying.
We find the stable master outside the stable waiting for us with two horses. Leilani must have called ahead.
" Good morning, your highness. It's good to see you." He greets me bowing. He stands at the flick of my hands.
I don't greet him back but I do nod my head in acknowledgement, it's tiring the good mornings I get in one day.
" Good morning Steve. I trust you have the horses ready for us." Leilani asks the man.
I am slightly embarrassed to say that I do not know his name but then again I don't know any of the servants or guards names except Leilani, Donavan and Mabel plus the ones Leilani introduced me to.
" I have everything ready for you, miss Adair. This here is Pegasus and Zeus. The best riding horses in the stable." He says referring to the horses.
Leilani smiles and goes over to pet them and I take a conscious step back.
I am not scared of horses, I just don't like them. They look at you like they can look straight into your soul. You have to trust them with your life, they can throw you off their backs anytime they want.
" Vaughn, you're going to have to come closer if you're going to ride Pegasus here." Leilani says, her voice filled with amusement.
Sighing I walk over and consciously pet Pegasus's mane.
The stable master looks at me with amusement but says nothing.
" Do you need help mounting?" Leilani asks me when she sees that I am not making any attempts to mount.
" No, I can do it myself." I answer her tersely.
She looks at me with a face that says do it, baiting me.
Fine.
I attempt to mount but misstep and fall miserably, landing on my ass.
I close my eyes at the pain and breathe in. Fuck that hurt.

" Need help getting up? Your highness." Leilani asks me, offering me a hand to help me stand up.

She looks like she wants to laugh but holds it in for the sake of my pride which right now is in bloody tatters.

She helps me stand up and I wince when I stretch because my ass took the brunt of that fall.

I close my eyes and concentrate on self healing because there's no bloody way I am going to ride with a sore ass.

" Do you need help mounting now?" She asks me again.

Swallowing my pride I nod my head and she indicates for Steve to come over.

He brings a stool with him that I use to get on Pegasus.

I close my eyes tightly when he moves beneath me but breathe sighing of relief when he stops fidgeting and gets used to my weight.

I look over at Leilani who mounts her horse with ease. Like she was born riding.

Her hair is in a messy braid and she looks beautiful in the morning sun.

Steve hands her a backpack and she guides her horse to stand besides mine.

" I hope you're better at riding than you're at mounting." She says.

" I am good at riding, I just haven't done it in a while. Father made sure I was able to ride by the time I was seven." All true but that doesn't change the fact that I simply don't like riding.

" Good. Then I guess you won't have trouble keeping up."

She urges her horse into a gallop before I can ask her what she means.

I urge Pegasus to trot at a much slower pace than Zeus and we slowly follow Leilani.

She rides out of the yard and stops just outside the gate.

" We have to get off this road and into the riding grounds so keep up." She says when I finally reach her.

I nod and she turns her horse towards a path I didn't even notice before considering it's opposite my gates.

This time around instead of galloping at a pace that has me fearing that she will break her neck, she trots beside me.
She's smiling as she rides.
" You must really like riding." I say to her,
" Really what gave it away?" She answers with a little sarcasm.
" Just a hunch I guess." I day with a smirk.
" I love riding, it was one thing I did a lot with my dad. I don't remember much about him but I remember riding with him." She says with a smile.
" I hate riding." I finally say.
" Really, I wouldn't have known had you not told me." She says feigning shock.
I chuckle and she joins in laughing.
" Why did you come if you hate riding, you realise I would have suggested we do something else right." She says,
We are now completely off the road and in a forest with riding paths.
" I know but you looked so fucking happy in your riding outfit that I didn't have ths heart to say no, besides spending the morning with you is worth all the heart attacks I am having because Pegasus keeps on trying to throw ms off his back." I mean it. She laughs,
" He is not trying to throw you off his back. Had he wanted to, you would already be on your ass." She says smirking.
" You are not making riding him any easier you know." I now hold the reins.
" I wasn't trying to," she smirks, " don't hold his reins tightly like that. He senses your fear."
See why I find them weird, it senses fear for fucks sake. I loosen my hold on the reins and we keep on riding.
We ride in silence for a few minutes, her enjoying the beautiful scenery and me looking at her, her smile, her hair.
We ride until we find a spot that offers privacy and has a place for the horses to rest.
She gets off her horse easily and guides him towards the sound of water. I do the same and follow her behind until we come out

on a little clearing with a small stream nearby.
She gets both horses and ties them so they can both graze and drink water without running away.
She gets the back pack that Steve gave her and removes a picnic blanket, spreading it down.
She takes a seat and I go to sit beside her. I slightly wince because my arse still hurts a little despite self healing.
" This place is beautiful, and peaceful." I say.
It really is, had I come here prepared, I would have come with paint and paint brushes so I could paint.
" It is, isn't it? I have been coming here since I was twenty. No one knows about it, it's so far off the paths that I am sure they are scared of wild animals or something." She says,
She hands me a bowl of fruit from her bag and a bottle of water.
" You came prepared, I see." I tease.
" Of course I did. I love food so much, plus I didn't have breakfast before leaving." She answers me,taking a sip of her water.
We watch the horses and eat our food.
" Do find these spots in the forests alot. This is a second one you have brought me to, not as breathtaking as the first but still."
I say, reminding her of the one she took me to after I started turning at the ball.
" I love to explore and I love nature so I am always looking for spots and places like this."
" How many of these little hidden places have you found so far?"
" Not many, be good and I will take you to all of them, your artistic side will go crazy."
" I'm already going crazy right now."
" You know you can take a picture and use that as reference when you get back right?"
" I do but believe it or not, the only thing or person I am interested in painting is you. When I hold a pencil or a brush and look at you, I find I have myself a dilemma because there alot of things about you I want to capture in the moment and very little time."
She smiles shyly for the first time, blushing.

" Has anyone ever told you that you have a way with words?" I laugh dryly,
" You are the first person to tell me that. Most people would go for the word broody. I talk the most when I am with you." I say,
" But I hear you talk, I mean you talk to Marshall."
" I do, mostly in a few sentences. I started talking more when I came back which is kind of ironic because u thought I might become mute again."
" The mute prince has done it again, he was seen leaving a hotel with not one but three ladies, how does he manage?" She says in a sarcastic voice, quoting a headline the media had once used.
" Ha ha, very funny." She laughs and almost chokes on a piece of apple.
" I am sorry it's just that, they made you look like some slimy dickhead or something. I was a little skeptical when I was asked to be, you know, your pretend 'mistress' due to all the headlines and stories I either read or heard." She admits.
For the first time since the mute prince headlines started circulating, I want to go back and change them even though not all of them were true.
" What changed your mind?" I ask her,
" You, when I met you at the airport despite your staring," she says, eying me, " You looked wounded. I saw the expression on your face when you disembarked from the plane, like you were being walked to your death." She says in a serious tone.
" I felt like that." I say sighing.
" Why?"
" Leilani the last time I was in Ambrosia, father packed me and a bunch of servants in a plane and took me to a kingdom I hardly knew. My mom had just died,I needed a father, I needed a family . What I got instead was king Ambrose. Shit like that messes children up no matter how strong they are."
She moves closer and squeezes my hold, letting me know she's here with me and I take comfort in that small gesture.
" Is that why you stopped talking?" She asks.
" Doing your research on me, are we?" I ask, looking at her.

" I like to be thorough, besides you hardly talk about yourself and I like you plus it's not a secret to you." She likes me.
When you put it like that, it only makes sense that she knows, I would have been suspicious if she didn't know.
" No, I went selectively mute after the death of my mom." I tell her.
I wait for her to say something but she says nothing, just squeezes my hand urging me to go on.
" I had been learning how to use my gift of healing. I hadn't had a break in two days and it was taking a toll on me. Father had decided that I should learn using roses. I had to learn because it was becoming hard to fake injuries especially when they healed within seconds. I can control them and they even take longer but I was fifteen then so it was hard. Father didn't want anyone to get suspicious so he started showing me how to use it." I stand up and pluck a flower near the stream before coming back to sit.
" You see healing is tricky and when you're just learning how to heal, it can be very messy."
I hold the flower in one hand and start to heal it.
It grows new leaves and the stem extends, the petals becoming larger and Leilani gasps softly at the sight.
" You see, when done right, this happens but," As soon as it started to grow and heal, the flower in my hands starts to dry up and die. It dies quicker than it healed, its petals drying up.
" The same hand that heals has the power to kill, especially when the healing isn't done right."
I heal the flower in my hands again until it is once again beautiful. I give it to Leilani.
" You see, I managed to kill maybe a hundred plus Rose's in those days. Father had selected that I use roses when learning because they were mom's favourite flower and using them would motivate me more." Cruel I know.
" After my second afternoon locked in a room, mom decided to sneak me out for some afternoon tea. So I could swim and get some fresh air and just be a boy or a teenager. I agreed reluctantly and went with my former keeper, Garrett. Mom was

there with her guard Leilani."

I swallow thickly, my emotions almost choking me.

" I was swimming, literally under water when I heard her scream. I heard shots ring out, like a forward I stayed underwater for longer than necessary and when I got put,I went straight to her. She was laying in a pool of her own blood. I couldn't see straight, Lei. I tried to heal her but I couldn't. I almost fucking changed right there in front of all the other guards, I had to be knocked out for me to be taken inside."

Leilani is now kneeling in front of me, hugging close to her chest as sobs wrack my body. All the sorrow I kept inside for so long, held on a tight leash. It's like a dam has cracked and all my emotions,my anger, my sorrow, they are all finally coming out.

" I haven't been to her gravesite since you know, I killed her. Had I held my ground and said no, she would still be alive, Garrett and Leilani would still be here but I couldn't hold my ground. I killed her." I say, tears falling down my cheeks.

" You did not kill her, Vaughn. Stop carrying all this guilt around, you didn't kill her and I am sure wherever she is, she agrees with me."

I say nothing. We spend the rest of the picnic or what's left of it there until I come down then ride back to my house.

Chapter 13

Edward Vaughn

After our little picnic and horse riding morning out, I have spent very little time with Leilani.
Duty calls and all that.
The last three weeks have been a blur of meetings and work.
I am always with Leilani Leilani because she is my keeper and all that but it's mostly in front of people and usually work related so we barely talk.
I just landed from my trip to one of the independent islands I plan on helping once I am king and I am tired.
What I want to do is get home,have a warm meal and get a hot bath and maybe sleep even if it's for a few hours before my nightmares start.
I don't wait for anyone to open the door when the car is parked.
I didn't travel with Leilani this or Marshall for the first time in a really long time so I haven't seen them in a week.
I don't see either of them anywhere, something I expected from Marshall because the man is a hermit and only leaves his room when it suits him.
" Bring my food up to my room." I tell a maid passing by.
She nods and runs to do as I have told her.
I get to my room and find the living room outside my room empty. I am tempted to check if Leilani is in her room but I fight the urge and decide to at least bathe and eat before seeing her.
I take off my shirt and sit down to take off my shoes when the

door opens.
I feel her before I see her.
I turn around and look at her, praying she's not a mirage and that she won't disappear before my eyes.
She looks beautiful, better than when I last saw her but maybe that's just because I haven't seen her in a long time.
" Staring is rude." She says with a smile.
" Fuck been rude, Lei I will stare at you untill my eyes can't see anything anymore but I won't care because you will be the last thing I see." I tell her, walking towards her.
" You do have a way with words." She says standing on her tiptoes to kiss me.
I lift her against me and kiss her like that's my last act on earth.
She sighs into my mouth and I groan because fuck it all, I missed her.
I push her against the wall,my hunger and fatigue of but forgotten though I am starving for something else entirely.
There's a knock on the door and she tries to stop kissing me but I don't let her go.
" Come in and leave the food on the table."
I shout.
" Vaughn no, what if they see us. You might not know this but maids are the notorious gossipers around." She says in my head.
The door opens and I still have her against the wall but the maids don't see us, they leave my food and leave without seeing us.
" Fuck, I forgot about your tricks." She says once the door is closed behind the maids.
" You always do, Lei. I missed you and I am starving for you, one kiss won't cut it with you because I want you so much."
I say against her, my cock hard against her stomach.
" Wait but I also can't see you, does that mean you can't see me as well?" She asks me, fascinated with the fact that we are invisible.
" Really Lei, of all the things I have said, that's all you can ask."
I ask her.
This woman, only she would ask such a thing when I have her against the wall and I am hard as fuck.

" I am genuinely curious, like what if we fucked naked, how would you see me." She ask again.
I don't say anything as I carry her towards the bed. I put her down and spread her knees, kneeling between them.
" Lei I know your body better than I know mine, I don't have to see you to fuck you when I can feel you."
If I could see her right now, I am sure she would be smiling.
" Take off your dress." I tell her.
I am not sure if she does. The only downside to fucking her when we are both invisible is the fact that I can't see her naked, or see her eyes when she comes.
" Done." She says and I see the dress appear on the floor since she's no longer wearing it, I can no longer make it invisible.
" Good." I say before using my hands to feel her body.
I find her breasts and pinch them a little making her moan, the sound going straight to my already hard cock.
I bend and start kissing her from her breasts, following a path I can't see but can sense.
I kiss her body, worshiping her until I find her belly button.
I kiss it and move lower, I feel her panties against my chin and move until I am directly in front of her wet core.
I kiss her against her panties and she moans.
" Well look what my exploring found. Honey dew, sweet and warm." I say still pressing light kisses against her panties.
She moans, lifting her hips against my mouth.
" Patience love, you asked me how we would make this work and I want to make sure your question gets answered."
I continue kissing her lightly.
" Vaughn if you don't fuck me right now, I will leave an even bigger mark in you with my dagger this time around." She says, threatening me.
" So violent, love." I say, moving her panties to the side but still only kissing her lightly.
" Vaughn please." She begs me.
" I like you begging. Please what?" I ask her teasing. I suck on her clit once and she groans and I go back to kissing her lightly.

" Please fuck me, Vaughn please." She pleads again.
" Fuck you with what Lei, you're going to have to be more specific than that." I say.
" With your mouth Vaughn, please fuck me with your mouth." She screams. I am glad that the guards in the corridors can't hear her because I don't want them hearing her scream and moan when I have her.
" My pleasure." I say before ripping her panties off her body.
I throw them to the floor and start to lick and suck on her clit like a man fucking starved.
I bite her a little and auck on her to soothe the bite sting.
I eat her out until I feel her start to tighten before sliding two of my fingers into her. I fuck her with my fingers and my mouth and she comes.
I don't stop licking and sucking until she rides her wave out.
" Fuck." She says her voice is hoarse.
" Does that answer your question?" I ask her teasing.
I turn off my gift and see her laying on her back breathing hard, her lips swollen from all my kissing and her body flushed from coming.
" Wow." She says sitting up.
She pushes me on my back and our positions are reversed. She unzips my jeans and pulls then down with my boxer briefs.
She grabs my cock, making me groan.
" Fuck, Lei."
" What?" She asks me innocently as she grips me hard and starts moving her hand up and down.
I almost come because fuck it, it feels so damn good.
Her other hand moves to my balls as the other grips me. She's so good at what she is doing that I don't even want to know how she got so good.
Moves forward bringing my cock to her lips,
" No love, you don't have to..."
I don't get to finish my statement before she has me in her mouth.
I groan and try not to come.

She takes me in her mouth until I hit the back of her throat and starts moving her head.
I stay transfixed watching her, her hair a mess around her.
She pushes me to the back of her throat and starts making a weird humming sound which I feel from my cock to my toes and I come so fucking hard.
Leilani swallows every last drop of my cum, milking me until I have nothing left to give before she sits up.
" You're amazing." I say.
" Thank you, now get up, you have to bathe and eat. You must be tired."
I don't argue with her because I am really tired but I insist that she showers and eats with me.
We fuck in the shower and she scratches my back, a mark I wear with pride.
After eating I plead with her to spend the night with me and after a lot of reluctance she agrees.
I sleep with her pressed against me.

I don't remember the last time I slept like this, no nightmares. Just peacefully, a seamless I appreciate.
Leilani mumbles something in her sleep, something I don't understand.
She starts shaking,the same thing I do when I have my nightmares and continues mumbling.
I sit up to look at her.
She looks restless and I know that whatever she is dreaming about isn't good.
I am about to wake her up when I am pushed off the bed with so much force that I am sure I will crack a bone.
I quickly stand up to check on Leilani and almost pass out.
" You're a keeper?" I all but scream.

Chapter 14

Leilani

I had been having one of my nightmares. All I know is that he was there trying to kill me like he had my parents but I fought back and escaped.
I transformed in my dream which led to me transforming in my sleep and pushing Vaughn off the bed.
" You're a keeper." He says looking at my wings.
My eyes are probably violet as well so I can't exactly lie to get out of this one.
" I never said I wasn't." I answer him simply.
" You know what I fucking mean Leilani, I thought the last of the true keepers died."
By that he means Garret, my father.
" They did." I say.
He walks towards me. I expected him to be upset or something but he looks anything but upset.
" How?" He asks, trying not to touch my wings.
" Garret was my father." I say simply.
" Shit." He says, closing his eyes.
He sits down on the bed with his head in his hands.
There's a reason I chose not to tell anyone who my parents had been.
It was mostly because I was scared for my life, who ever killed my dad would kill me the moment he knew what I was so in his who I was.

I change back, putting my wings back inside and wince.
It never gets any easier removing them and putting them back in.
" Does it hurt?" Vaighn asks me, now looking at me.
" Like a bitch. My skin opens and closes around them in order to accommodate them." I say with a smile.
" Why didn't you tell me?"
" I wanted to. No one knows that I am a true keeper but you."
" Why not?"
" I am not yet ready. Please don't tell anyone, at least not yet."
I sit down next to him.
" I would never betray you like that, Lei, whatever your reasons for not telling anyone I respect them." He says.
" Thank you. This means a lot to me." I say.
I have to keep my identity a secret for the time being because he is still in a position of power and can have me killed.
" You looked like an angel, with your wings and everything." He says in a light voice.
" Thank you. Grams said the same thing when I learnt how to fly."
" I would love to see you fly." He says.
" Maybe someday you will."
" Do you also get nightmares?" He asks me after some time.
" Yeah, sometimes."
He stands up and gets me a bottle of water from the fridge in the living room outside his room.
He pulls me against him, cuddling me and covers us with a blanket.
" What causes them?" He asks me.
" When I turned fifteen, I somehow started to see the last moments of dad's life."
He freezes, everything in his body going still.
" What do you mean the last moments of his life?"
" The last moments before he died. I used to see it, like a twisted movie on replay. The queen getting shot, mom running over and her getting shot as well, dad looking for the threat but not being

able to defend his wife or his queen then getting shot."
I say, my throat closing up.
" Leilani was your mother, of course. Fuck, angel I am so sorry. I don't know what else to say." He says, kissing the top of my head.
" It's okay, it wasn't your fault. It was their time to die, at least they lived a great life."
Father lived the best life, he may not have been able to see me grow but he was happy. Every now and then, I get a glimpse into his memories to see the life he lived. He was happy, one of my favourite memories is the one when he took me riding. I had just learnt how to sit and I may not be able to remember it but I know he was happy so I take joy in knowing that.
" How come no one knew about your parents being together. They acted like strangers around each other."
" They liked to keep their life private."
He nods and says nothing for some time.
" You cheated, angel." He says in an excited voice all of a sudden.
" What do you mean cheated?" I ask him.
" That day in the gym, you absorbed my powers. That's why you got so freakishly strong."
" That or maybe I am simply strong, hasn't that thought occurred to you."
" Or you just cheated." He says laughing.
He pulls me close and hugs me.
" Sleep angel, you are not alone."
Angel,I like that.

I don't see much of Vaughn the next morning and Marshall. He's gone to the castle for a meeting with the king.
That scares me a bit but I trust him completely so I don't pay much attention.
By midday he still isn't back so I get my bike and get ready to go for a ride.
I am about to leave when I see Reginald coming over.
" Going out?"
" Yeah, I need some time to myself."

" Does he know?"
" Know about what?" I ask him, confused.
" Did he find out that you're a keeper?"
I look at him surprised because like I told Vaughn last night, no one knows about me.
" How do you know?" I ask him.
I love Reginald like a brother, I always have but if it came to taking him out I would do so in a heartbeat.
" Can't tell you that but just know that I haven't told anyone else. My loyalty lays with you."
I look at him skeptical
" Trust me. Go for your ride, I will remain here and keep guard but Leilani, war is coming, be ready."
He leaves before I can say anything. Fuck my life.

Riding had taken me to the first place I had brought Vaughn when he had been having a hard time at the party.
I parked my bike and spent the rest of the day reading.
I love reading because it's one of the things that make my life seem normal as compared to everything else around me.
I get up and start getting ready to go back when I hear a faint whimpering sound.
I look for where the sound is coming from and see a tiny ball of fur near the trees.
I move closer and find that it's a tiny world pup, it's white fur tinged with blood.
I pick it up gently, making sure not to hurt it more than it already is. Fuck, where's Vaughn when you need him.
" Lei, angel!" Someone shouts.
Speak of the devil.
" I am here." I shout back.
Minutes later, I hear his footsteps.
" I have been looking for you, did you get hurt or something?"
" Not me, him or her, I don't know."
I say, showing him the pup who is still whimpering.
" What's wrong with it?"

" I am not sure, just heard it whimpering and found it."
" Here, give it to me."
I hand him the pup and he holds it gently and like he always does, I watch his hands light up like fireflies as he heals it.
The pup stops whimpering and starts letting out a little howl and I smile.
" Thank you." I say when he finally puts it down.
" You don't have to thank me, you know that right?" I nod and kiss him.
The wolf pup starts licking my fingers and I laugh.
" Looks like you got yourself a new admirer." He tells me, looking at the pup.
" Can I keep him, I mean I want to but it's your house and what not."
" Yes you can keep him besides I am sure he was left here to die but his mother because of whatever happened to him."
I nod and pick him up.
" What are you going to call him?" He asks me.
" Phoenix, because he has been reborn."
" Good name."

Chapter 15

Leilani

Vaughn has known the truth about who I am for some days now and so far everything has been going fine.
We hang out though that's mostly me pretending to guard him and him cornering me and trying to get in my pants not that I mind.
He's told me about how he met Marshall and we have also gone out with Marshall three times.
Marshall is a nice person, I have always thought so despite his constant flirting which he stopped after he knew about me and Vaughn thankfully.
Phoenix the wolf pup I now own, who is a boy pup has been a pain in the ass to train but I love him so i guess that's ok.
For the first time since the death of grams, I am well and truly happy.
My negative thoughts have been getting the best of me though, because everytime you are happy, something bad is bound to happen, I just hope it isn't so.

" Come on." Vaughn says,
" I really don't want to."
" Angel it's a surprise, one I have been working on for days you just have to come."
" How far is it?" I ask him.
He has been asking me to come and see his surprise for the last ten minutes. As much as I have loved spending time with him

these past days, the man is engaged and yes me sleeping with him while knowing this was a bitch love on my part but still.
" It's within the house so it's not far, come on."
I follow him reluctantly.
We go through the house until we reach the west wing, a part of the house that is never in use.
" Close your eyes." He tells me when we come to stand at a certain part in the corridor. There are no doors in sight but I close my eyes without questioning him.
I hear a click and something has been pushed open before being guided into a room.
" Open your eyes."
I do as I am told and gasp. Wow.
My eyes fill with tears because wow.
" Do you like it?" He asks me nervously.
I am at a loss of words so all I do is nod.
He painted and drew pictures of me, most of them are like realistic photos of him he took at a certain time when we were together like the might of the ball, or the night he first saw me with my wings but it has been painted.
A whole room of paintings and drawings of me.
" I hope you don't find it creepy." He says.
" Are you kidding Vaughn this is the nicest thing anyone has ever done for me, thank you so much." I say crying because it really is the sweetest thing anyone has ever done for me.
" You're welcome plus it was my pleasure doing it."
I walk around looking at the paintings,one in particular when my eyes had turned violet and one when I had been dancing at the bar.
This man is truly talented.
" Angel, there's something I need to tell you." He says after some time.
" What is it?" I ask him.
Before he can say anything his phone rings and he picks up.
" Yes father."
I watch him,

" Ok I will be right there." He puts the phone back in his pocket and looks at me.
" I am sorry, duty calls. I still need to talk to you."
" It's okay, you will find me when you get back." I say.
He looks at me for a second.
" It's times like this that I wish I can read your thoughts and not just what you want me to see."
I smirk,
" Go I, you will find me when you get back."
We leave together and I notice that the room he took me in is hidden, you can only find it if you know it's there.

Chapter 16

Edward Vaughn

I find father's driver already waiting for me outside the house.

I am frustrated because I was with Leilani, I was going to tell her how I feel but of course duty calls as always.

I get into the car and the driver drives me to the castle.

When I get to the castle, I go straight to father's office and find him waiting for me.

Donavan and Conrad are with him and they bow in greeting, I nod once and take a seat.

" You called me father." I say.

He hasn't looked up to whatever he is doing since I came in.

" Yes I did. Princess Madison is coming in two days time with her father king Jonathan to finalise your engagement."

I look at him stunned.

" Why are you looking at me with that expression on your face, you have known about your engagement for months now."

I say nothing, just keep looking at him.

" Edward you realise that you need to marry this girl before you ascend right?"

I don't answer him or say anything for that matter.

I just leave his office, banging the door shut behind me.

Some of my guards who had followed me behind fall in step behind me.

Fuck him and his stupid rules.

Had he asked me to marry Madison when I first arrived back, I would have without questioning him but not now.
Not now that I am in love with Lei, not now.
I am too upset to go home right now so I go and visit the only other person who brought me peace.

I haven't been to the royal cemetery since mom was buried. I haven't attended any of her memorial services or bothered to send flowers.
Mostly due to guilt but also because I was too ashamed to show my face here but today I have come back here because no matter what happens I will always be her son and her my mother.
All my guards remained just outside in order to give me much needed privacy, something I appreciate.
I walk over to her tombstone and sit next to it.
" Hey mom. I brought roses. You probably don't want to hear from me but I had to come to you because I have nowhere else to go. I miss you and I am sorry for abandoning you, for trying to make it seem like you never existed. It's just that mom, it was too much. The pain was unbearable and I couldn't take it. The pain of losing you was too much, it hurt both physically and mentally so I did what I thought was best. I shut you out and I am sorry. For what happened to you. I want to say for not saving you but a very special someone told me that it wasn't my fault and for the first time in forever I believed her. You would love her mom, she's outgoing, caring and loving. She gave me the will to live in a long fucking time an before you say ' such language is unbecoming of a prince ' I am sorry. She's the best and mom I love her, I really do but now I have to choose between her and a future I have been promised since birth. I came here for help,I wanted someone to listen to me."
I say nothing else as I sit there.

I spend the night there trying to find peace.
Early in the morning I know what I must do so I go back home. Guards must have changed while I was at the cemetery because the ones I came with aren't the ones that drives me back but I don't pay much attention, to busy making plans for the future.

Chapter 17

Leilani

I am having breakfast with Marshall when Vaughn walks in looking worse for wear.

I haven't seen him since he left yesterday.

He walks straight to me.

" Come with me." I am about to say no but he pulls me up and starts to drag me behind him.

" Vaughn, what is wrong with you?"

He doesn't stop until we reach one of the cars parked outside,

" Get in." I get in not because I want to but because he is dragging me out all but making us a two man show because everyone is watching us.

He gets into the driver's seat and drives us out of the yard.

" Vaughn what the fuck is wrong with you? You just left your security behind."

" I want to talk to you alone, I don't want them around. Trust me, please."

I keep quiet after that. He drives us to the spot where I found Phoenix and parks the car there.

He unbulckes his and my seat belts and turns to look at me.

" I need to tell you something."

" That's the reason you all but dragged me out during breakfast. What is wrong, I haven't seen you since yesterday."

I am upset but mostly worried because that's what this man does to me.

" I went to see father then spent the night at the royal cemetery with mom."

" Vaughn, honey,are you ok?"

" Question of the decade, that one." He says, sighing.

" I went there to ask her for forgiveness and to seek advice on something and I am happy to tell you that I found what I had been looking for."

" What is it you had been looking for?" I ask him.

He looks at me,

" Don't say anything until I finish speaking." He says and I nod in agreement.

" Lei since the death of my mom I have suffered and struggled so much, if it wasn't for the fact that I am immortal I would have killed myself to rid myself of this suffering," I hold his hand, squeezing slightly knowing what he means.

" I used to get upset when I saw people that were genuinely happy or in love, that was until I saw you in that tiny dress of yours at the airport. I tried to hide from you because you made me feel things that scared me but against my better judgement I would seek you out. I tried to fight it but the love I have for you was simply too much," I feel tears gather in my eyes but I keep quiet.

" I have tried looking at other women but none of them compare to you. Having you in my life these last few weeks has brought me nothing but joy, that I am willing to forget about Madison and my royal obligations, you have shown me what love is like, what true happiness is where others failed. Fuck traditions angel, fuck the throne because I have never met anyone like you and letting you go will be like slowly killing myself."

I am now silently crying because that is the most beautiful thing anyone has ever said to me.

" People that want love are a lot in this world, but only few of them are able to find it. Lei you have my heart and my soul, to do with as you please give me yours and I will protect you from anything the world throws your way. I will love you till my dying day and will do so with every part of my being." I squeeze his

hand again,
" Angel you have melted me and all the walls that I had built around my heart, I have grown that my heart now knows the difference between right and wrong. Take me, Lei, I am yours and will always be yours."
He looks at me and I try to speak but can't because God the first time in my life I have been rendered speechless.
I am about to say something when I feel a sharp piercing pain go through my chest.
I look down and see blood then look up to Vaughn's stunned expression then everything goes black.

Edward Vaughn

Fuck fuck fuck, not again.
Shots ring out around us and I am not sure who is shooting at us or why all I know is that I have to save Lei no matter what.
The bullet made a clean cut through her chest so all i have to do is heal her.
I pull her close to me and start healing, using all the power I can master because if she dies, I will die with her.
I feel a sharp pain at the back of my head but don't bother inspecting it.
I will check on it later but only after I confirm that my angel.is breathing.
I heal her until all the power is drained out of me and I only stop when I see her chest start rising and falling before passing out.

Chapter 18

Ambrose

" Where is he?" I ask the foolish keeper in front of me.
" In his old chambers, your majesty."
I head there followed closely behind by my royal adviser Levine.
The stupid boy, love has always made him weak, it was one of the reasons I had his stupid mother and keeper killed but no that wasn't enough, he had to go and fall in love again and this time with his body guard.
I open the door and find him in bed, his face deathly white.
" Why isn't he awake?" I ask Levine.
" He took a bullet to the head, your majesty." Of course he did.
" Still, he should have healed by now."
" Of course, your majesty."
" And his alut of a keeper, what about her?"
" She's back at his house, your majesty."
How the heck did she survive, she was supposed to have died today, I made sure of it.
" How did she survive?"
I know I made my instructions quite clear, a bullet through the heart.
" Prince Edward must have healed her, your majesty."
My son will never amount to anything in life with his weakness.
I can heal him but when he wakes up, I want to make sure he has no memories of his little keeper.
" Call Donavan."

" Yes, your majesty."

The door opens and Donavan steps in.

" Donavan."

" Yes, your majesty."

" Kill the keeper and make sure that everything about her vanishes, make sure she never existed."

" Excuse me."

" Did I stutter, make sure she never existed. And Donavan,"

" Yes, your majesty."

" Don't make any mistakes."

He nods before leaving and I turn to Levine.

" You, write down the memory loss spell."

" But your majesty, it's too dangerous a spell too powerful."

" Well then it's a good thing I am the one doing it."

Yes, everything will go back to normal soon enough.

Chapter 19

Leilani

I wake up screaming. Where's Vaughn and how am I awake? A bullet went straight through my heart.

I wake up in my room with Reginald, Marshall and Klara all looking at me.

" Where's Vaughn?"

" Back at the castle, don't worry he is healing and will be fine but you have to leave immediately."

" What do you mean to leave, I want to see Vaughn to make sure he is okay." I say getting up.

It's only after I stand that I see that there are bags packed like we are travelling somewhere.

" What's going on?" I ask confused as fuck though I am not the only one who looks confused because Marshall looks stunned as well.

" I have ears everywhere and the king just ordered someone to kill you, to erase you because he is going to wipe the prince's memory. Now I don't know about him," Reginald says pointing at Marshall, " But all I know is that I have a task and that's to keep you alive and safe."

" Why would he want me dead?" I wonder aloud,

" He doesn't know who I am or rather what I am. This isn't making any sense."

" None of this makes sense but we have to leave now,we need a safe heaven right now and standing here arguing about it is

wasting time." Klara says for the first time since I woke up.
I nod and start following them out the door.
" I will come with you, I have a safe haven we can go to."
Reginald agrees and we all leave.
We get into the first empty car we find and start driving to the airport.
" Why drive to the airport? We need a plane to leave." Klara asks Reginald.
" I have a plane that can get us out of here within the next hour." Marshall says.
Everything is happening so fast that I can hardly register what is happening around me.
The car stops in the middle of the road all of a sudden.
" I won't hurt you, all I want is Leilani then you can all go free." A voice outside says or rather Donavan's voice, ons that I know so well.
" We can take him, his alone so killing him will be quite easy." Klare says. She's never liked him so her suggestion comes as no surprise.
" No, killing him will only lead Ambrose to us. I Have an idea but you have to trust me." I say,
" I don't agree with.." I get out of the car before Reginald can finish talking.
" Leilani, fuck." He says frustrated as he follows me out.
Donavan smiles, his expression sardonic,
" Well well well, this won't be long, just one bullet and then nothingness." He says sarcastically, aiming the gun at me.
" I command you to put your gun down, Donavan."
He laughs snidely,
" You don't command me Leilani, I command you or have you forgotten."
" I haven't forgotten anything but then it seems you have, after all a true keeper born or keeper blood outranks a keeper picked by his king." He stops smiling and looks at me,
" What's this nonsense about a true keeper? We all know Garret was the last of them and he died years ago."

I smile and release my wings, my eyes turning violet.
" Think again."
He falls to one knee and bows, so does Reginald and Klara who get out of the car.
Marshall faints.
When you join the royal guard or become a keeper, we vow to protect our kings and masters but most importantly we vow to protect our own.
I am the last true keeper, meaning I am their first master.
" How?" Donavan asks me while still kneeling.
" Garret was my father. I don't have time to stand here and chat, find a solution to your king's dilemma and make sure he believes that you killed me and I will be out of your hair."
He nods and stands up before driving away.
" What a coward." Reginald says standing up.
" He knows you could kill them with the snap of your fingers so he run away. Also your wings look so freaking awesome." Klara says, making me genuinely smile for the first time since I woke up.
I see a motorcycle approach us but when Reginald makes no move to run I stand knowing it isn't a dangerous visit.
The bike parks and Mabel gets off with Phoenix who runs to me, leaking my legs.
" Are you here to finish the job your brother couldn't complete?" I ask her.
Mabel is a good person, she just isn't my good person, we have never gotten along and are both hello-good friends.
" Oh you didn't tell her?" She asks Reginald.
" Tell me what?" I am feeling confused.
" Well you see." Klara starts to explain.
" Keepers are either born of keeper blood or chosen when a new royal is about to be born and we just happen to be the chosen."
" Whose we and how this fuck are you chosen, you said it yourself you need a child to be born of royal blood."
" Us three. Me, Reggie and Mabel." Klara says softly.
" Ok good for you but then you still need children born of royal

blood."
" We already do, three of them to be precise. Baking in their mummy's tum tum." Mabel says in a sarcastic voice.
" Who?" I ask, still very confused.
" You. You're pregnant."
Fuck.
I see the ground getting closer then everything goes black.

Thank you so much for reading a court of dead roses.

Don't miss The Gifted Bloodlines Series Book Two- A Bokay Of White Phoenixes.

www.ingramcontent.com/pod-product-compliance
Lightning Source LLC
LaVergne TN
LVHW010105170826
845678LV00012B/2252

* 9 7 9 8 8 4 9 4 2 1 3 4 6 *